I0665389

the **first** time
she **fell**

the **first** time she **fell**

stories by Caleb Ludwick

C R PRESS

Published by in the United States by C&R Press. Early versions of the texts of "Swim" and "Underlay" were published online. For information address C&R Press at CRPress.org.

This is a work of fiction. Any resemblance to actual persons, living or dead, or events is entirely coincidental; names, characters, places and incidents are the product of the author's imagination or are used fictitiously. Some liberties have been taken with geography and locales altered or renamed.

ISBN 978-1-936196-28-9
LCCN 2013947232

In partnership with Eco-Libris, 100 trees have been planted toward the creation of this book. For more about Eco-Libris and making reading more sustainable, visit www.ecolibris.net.

to kgl

My in-love, promise me yourself,
And then forgetting that, remember me –
Me? Forget remembering that, then, and
Love my promise, yourself in me.

contents

I first met Bessie Smith in Orléans, France, on a turntable in my graduate school library. As I listened to her for the first time, her words shining on the scratch of a needle, I remember feeling ashamed that she was from my hometown of Chattanooga, Tennessee – not ashamed of her, but of myself. That I had lived for years within five miles of where she found her voice, and I had never heard her sing.

But when I returned to the U.S., I forgot. Diving headfirst into helping build the progressive reputation of the new New South, I worked with design agencies to create brands for arts organizations, environmental activists, revitalization programs, corporations, even City Halls. However, there was always a voice, quiet in the back of my head, and it was hers. Like so many blues masters, she calls to anyone who will listen to open the eyes of our eyes, to home. And when I listened, she led me into unexpected places and remarkable lives of people we had ignored, neglected, and even excluded in our rush to progress.

In response, I wrote "Thin King Blues," a verse story where a character named Bess speaks the lyrics from Ms. Smith's 1929 Columbia recording of "Thinking Blues," and a fictional narrator does his best to keep up. That story sparked other stories of imagined characters who propel themselves into situations where everything changes, of how they embrace or avoid themselves, and why, and what happens next.

My secret hope, I think, was that writing these stories would let me see life from other points of view. A naive hope, at best. Instead, they did what fiction does so well: creating momentary glimpses of empathy over apathy, of love over indifference, of a good word.

Thanks to a grant from the Lyndhurst Foundation, these stories became a collaborative art project with 8 graphic designers around the country, each of whom visually interpreted one of the pieces for a short run print book. And now, thanks to C&R Press, the edited stories are gathered and published as a collection.

Or, as I think of it, as a love letter – sometimes sharp, but always tender – to the many Souths that make up home.

cl, 2013

the **first** time
she **fell**

EVEN IN THE LATE COOL of a Saturday, the kitchen is hot as noon. Buckley walks through the swinging doors and sees her flushed at the open ovens, flour ribboning the light from the window. He stops short, wondering if she might take him by the hand and lead him along leafy streets to a first-floor efficiency, her backward glance insolent, secret, unafraid.

He says her name, and then something about maids, and waitresses, and servant girls; that she is wearing that apron like an invitation. And Marinela Constancia Ruiz hears him.

What Marinela didn't say:

- that maybe it's better to make a bad choice for good reasons, than a good choice for bad reasons.

- that 'Fingers with wedding bands stir a bitter batter' was a favorite saying of her mother.

- that the reason her mother, Señora Immaculata Vegas Ruiz, broke the custom of perpetuating family names should be obvious. After all, her own mother's own mother had broken the custom first, naming Immaculata Vegas after the local chapel and the bright postcards of Las Vegas – with the disastrous result that Vegas had seven children by four different visiting American businessmen.

So Immaculata Vegas, believing that naming can go a long way in either direction, had named Marinela after the brand of her favorite store-bought pastry. Brown outside but inside white, she would say. You might look dark as chocolate and inside be white as sweet cream filling, but never forget you can't be both. That, in America, you will never be either.

· that she had overheard Buckley's father tell him to clear dishes. His exact words (Marinela has an excellent memory) were: "Despite the presence of hired help, the groom should be host, sponsor and servant – all things to all people." So when Buckley pushed through the swinging doors with plates for the sink, she knew he was there not because he is a gentleman, but because he is a child.

· that she saw him stop resenting his father the moment he saw her, sweating in her apron. He grinned at her as if they'd never met, as if the cracked and yellowed ceiling was about to collapse on him in a settling haze of happiness.

· isn't this a grand party? Look at the chairs pushed against the wall for dancing, and a cake with three tiers and enough icing to make anybody happy. Groomsmen pretending to be adults pretending to be teenagers; boys in cummerbunds cupping beers and smoking cigars and cursing, their Tennessee down-South mouths tonguing the words like bleached teeth – nothing like when Tampico boys talk rough and tumble. Boys in girls in bathrooms and coat closets, or snatching handfuls of food from warming trays. Their mothers in pastel, wide-brimmed hats that hang low over their eyes.

· 4 fresh mint sprigs, 2 shots Bookers, 1 t powdered sugar, 2 t water, crushed ice.

· that she speaks excellent English because she grew up five miles from Mexico's first Coca-Cola bottling plant (est 1926). That the Southern brown sugar bubble water is as much in her blood as his. But that sometimes it is better to pretend she can't *hablo ingles*. Or speaking, not understand. Or understanding, not really understand.

- that her apron might be stained, but the cloth is two layers of canvas with a waterproof fabric sewn between. So he need not worry about her blouse.

- welcome back to the Wilhoit Street Reception Hall. Though she scarcely has the right to welcome guests, it being only her second month. On the other hand, every man and woman coming into the kitchen notices only her, so she might as well be appointed welcoming committee.

- The two other cooks, Jaione and Jasmine, have each worked at the Hall for more than thirty years, while she herself is not thirty years old, or twenty-five, or even twenty-two. She had been hired just after Easter, when Miss Emmeline died, at the age of 81. From what the others say, Miss Emmeline suffered a stroke while driving home on the Interstate, her hands gripping the wheel of her Pontiac in a heroic act, steering her car out of traffic. Her car rolled to a standstill on the grass and gravel shoulder. The burning sun crept toward the tailgate. When the police arrived, they stopped only because the exhaust was spouting great clouds of dry smoke; they thought Miss Emmeline must be waiting for a grandchild who had gone to squat on his heels among the pines.

- that Easter is a wonderful holiday in America, whatever that business about the rabbit.

- that he reminds her of a man from Alabama, who came down to Tampico looking for low wage labor, who had dressed a hundred of them in print shorts and tank tops and boarded them onto a leased Carnival cruise ship. Sailed straight into the Puerto de Mobile smeared with sunscreen and coached on how to act drunk and entitled. Kids were given blow-up toys. Young mothers gagged infants and tucked them into hollow watermelons with tiny air holes, to keep the crying sounds inside, until they were reborn, sticky sweet, into America.

The border patrol was too busy hunting illegals to worry about a cruise ship of bitchy tourists, so they walked straight up Government Street and onto construction sites. But Marinela and her sisters and their mother kept walking all the way to the bus stop, all the way to Chattanooga. Following that brown bubble sugar water flowing like a lifeline between home and home.

· that on the long bus ride, her mother had gathered everyone together to say that she had no legacy to give, other than the ability to smile and endure with the passion and patience of a portrait. Saying that this is not how things should be, or could be, or perhaps even will be, only how they are.

· that her first week in Chattanooga, a man saw her in a Bi-Lo grocery and offered her the role of the Virgin, in an Easter parade. The parade was where she first saw Buckley, and shook his hand. He offered her a job in the Men's Grille at the golf club, but the following day, his fiancée arranged that she work, instead, at the Wilhoit Street Reception Hall.

· that she is an American, bona fide, with cartoon memories, a favorite toothpaste and a business plan, *muchas gracias*. That her children will have no accent, until they want one.

· that he knows full well that her apartment is not on a leafy street but off a short city bus line, down a brown path that winds through back yards to a cinder block building passed over by the revival of Main Street. No fraud-mod balustrades decorate her building. Only a few years before, the apartment was squatted by dry-skinned alcoholic prostitutes who bummed cigarettes from the insurance workers downtown; but then the university launched an aggressive student exchange program, and within six months a venture capital firm out of Knoxville bought the building on the cheap and filled it with lipsticked Japanese sophomores drinking Fresca and wearing tee shirts silkscreened with *MAYBE* or *CECI N'EST PAS SEXY*.

- that it's the little things that get us through, because nothing doesn't seem too much to ask. Tiny mountains can only have tiny avalanches.

- that when Buckley saw her at the Easter parade and wrote his cell phone number on her hand, she watched the ink spread into her palm's lines and creases like a future. Him, whose mother is Regent of the D.A.R., founder of the Junior League mentoring program, a Gold supporter of the Pops, Chair of the Christmas Silent Auction at the Y three years running. And her, whose mother is Señora Immaculata Vegas Ruiz. She had enjoyed imagining the two mothers together in the tiny apartment, over *chiles en nogada*, until she heard that in just two weeks he would be married. Her sister had called her common; but she, Constancia Marinela Ruiz, had said there is no shame in being common.

- that when he came into the dark hotel bar, tan from boating, from all that sun on all that water, the pale sunglasses circles around his eyes made him look as if he looked at the whole world in wonder. She had been suddenly aware of her knees showing under the brief skirt, small and vulnerable, of her black tee shirt tight across her chest, printed in block letters with *FEED ME. FUCK ME. FINANCE ME.*

And, in case he didn't remember,as he got drunk on tall cold bottles of beer, he was already talking about horses.

- that Jasmine keeps a hat rack locked in the corner of the kitchen pantry; the hats were all stolen, over the years, from guests drunk on sangria. The week before Marinela left with Buckley for the Derby, the three cooks pulled out the hats, choosing favorites in the burnished back of a pasta pot; made cucumber sandwiches and mixed juleps; placed bets on ants running the windowsill. Jasmine clapping her hands; Jaione's cheeks rosy with cracked capillaries by years of oven heat and envy. Marinela laughing, the sound rolling up from her belly to spill out of her mouth, as easy as breathing.

· that she had found the infield to be just like they say on the Internet. The Great Party of bourbon breath and blonde hair and round vowels, and thousands pressing in from every side, shouting and groping and passing out. Fireworks popping like synapses. Over by the third turn, boys were pulling girls down to mud wrestle beneath the always clean, perfectly set, immense hats of bows and pastels and live flowers and silk trim and feathers that made her sneeze.

And when the race started, it seemed that the whole world was shouting together, their voices twisted in the air, braiding together under the thunder of hooves. But then, too soon, came the finish. As silence spread across the track, she pushed through to the fence, away from his hand, and stood crushed against the railing while three men held the horse down. It tried to rise on shattered forelegs, blood dark as lipstick against the pale bone. Its eyes were wild with filly fright as the jockey turned and walked away, not wanting to see the veterinarian run, with his long needle, toward the vein. And voices all around Marinela said: she got second, she ran damn fine. She ran like a locomotive, like a veteran; she ran like a colt, like a muse.

· that she had walked straight to a bus stop and caught the long ride back to downtown Louisville, to Lexington, to Knoxville, to Chattanooga. That she had been in the reception hall kitchen the next morning, before the sun came up. That she had watched him get married through the window, through the cool slant of Saturday sun.

• that she is not a pastry or a muse or a mare or a virgin or a Friday night white flight or Saturday stalker or *enamorada* or *chucha cuerera* or clutch or squeeze or flame or crush. That she is only a woman waiting for him to leave, so she can go into the pantry to choose today's favorite hat. To laugh over the oven heat until tiny veins in her face pop, blushing.

So when Buckley is standing by the sink, watching as she washes plates, Marinela hears him talking, but she is not listening. And when he says, "It doesn't have to change. She doesn't have to know. You could come downtown with me tomorrow night. The men would bow, the women blush," Marinela's pretty face screws up into a question mark, and she says nothing.

swim

OUR MOTHER drowns in Alabama, off a white sand beach. Gabby and I are wading knee-deep, hunting shells with our toes. We compare them side-by-side on flat palms before Gabby shouts, "Back you go," and throws them winking into the surf. I lower mine slowly, waiting for the current to twitch them alive in my fingers, to whip them away. It's a long time before we notice that Mom is gone.

The police station is a big room of hard concrete and beat-up metal teachers' desks. Everything is dusty and everybody is wearing dark blue uniforms. A man is talking to me, swallowing over and over, his Adam's apple thumping up and down, and Gabby won't stop crying, her eyes and nose and mouth spreading wet across a woman's shirt. Out the window I see piers and restaurants, and families playing on towels that are spread out like blankets on the sand, and hotels with stacked balconies. Yesterday Dad told me that the prices of the hotel room go up as the floors go up, because they're selling views of the waves. I haven't heard Dad say anything since this morning.

The airline upgrades our seats to first class for the flight home. At the check-in, white people stare and whisper at us, like Arabs and airplanes can't play nice. I want to pull the hijab closed around my face, to hide my dark skin and eyes so they can go back to forgetting about us. But then Dad buys three tiny bottles of whiskey from the duty free, and people decide we must be good Americans, and stop staring. Dad pours the whiskeys into a plant when nobody is looking.

Soon, Dad is soon snoring beside me with Gabby tucked under his shoulder, in tight, like dads always do. Inside the airplane, everything is cool and dry, closed in. It reminds me of hide and seek, of the air conditioning vent under my bed.

The stewardess comes by wearing a suit jacket that is buttoned all the way up to her smile.

"You want a Coke, honey?" she asks, bending very close so as not to wake Dad and Gabby. "It's free. It comes with the ticket."

I know better than to wake Dad up and ask if it's okay He would say, things that pollute in large amounts in small amounts are haram. He would also say, look at the miseries whiskey has brought mankind, the sin greater than the profit. So says the prophet. But look at him now, three bottles gripped in his knuckles. The appearance of evil.

Maybe, in first class, the rules change. I want them to, because I've heard that Coke has caffeine, and I don't want to sleep, to dream about waves white capped for miles, about Mom winking at me from the surf, her eyelids tumbled shells.

"Will caffeine impair my judgment?" I ask the stewardess. Her face is soft under her makeup.

"What a big girl question," she says, and I can feel her words on my cheek. "You are a big girl. You're going to be okay."

We come home in the early morning, before the sun is up. We drive Broad Street with its Bradford pears and parking meters glowing like summer Christmas lights, past the new, bright and shining theater where we've never been, and the marble white buildings with long flags sighing in the dark.

As we turn onto Central Ave I see yellow backhoes with unAmerican-sounding names being unloaded from their trailers. Crews have been digging through the street while we were gone, and chunks of black tar and dirt are piled like dog poop on the sidewalk. Men in reflective vests and hard hats are shading their eyes against the bright work lights, peeking into the holes they've dug. The machines work the dirt, tick tock, a few feet deeper. Soon, all the cars in the neighborhood will back out of driveways for school or work, the drivers' faces swinging past the holes in the street, going slow, curious, stretching their necks to see what is being buried or uncovered, suspicious of everything.

In my room, I heave my suitcase onto my bed and fish in my closet for my basketball. Out in my driveway, the gravel grinds under my shoes.

The cold light from the work crews bends around houses, shining on the driveway and the duct tape free throw line, and the backboard mounted high and rusting on the side of the shed.

Mom used to practice with me here. She was no good, always out of breath and wanting a break, but she'd reach around my hips, bump me, block my shots.

"You're not supposed to block your daughter."

"Says who?"

"But, you're the mom."

"Don't say, The Mom. How can I live up to that?"

I'd laugh and she would slap at the ball like she didn't know how to steal it. I don't want to think about that, or about men digging through the street, uncovering pipes. About Mom coming apart slowly in the Gulf, bits of her working their way upstream into Tennessee rivers, to trickle under city streets. I want to imagine her scattered in stars, reflected over the ocean. But I can't.

Dad appears in the kitchen doorway, rolling up his sleeves.

"Sure you don't want to sleep a bit?" he asks me.

I bounce him the ball.

"Gabby won't either. And now your Teta is awake and cooking lentils, and saying we never should have moved to a city where we have no family to cook for us. The whole house stinks like onions."

I don't want to look at him, not now, unshowered and with his face unshaven, his glasses smeared, starting another day in the same clothes. He squeezes the basketball between his hands. I point at the rim.

"There are so many things for me to do," he said.

"Just ten minutes?"

We take turns shooting, the ball bright in the fake light from the street. My throws are all short but he rebounds for me, taking his long steps back to the taped line. At first he is clumsy, distracted, his feet blind on the gravel, but then the ball finds a rhythm with the sounds of morning – dogs barking, machines eating up the ground.

I try to listen to his breathing between each bounce, the ball and breathing together in a way that seems to be saying something I can't hear over my own heartbeat. And then, as the driveway turns into day around us, he dribbles between his legs and steps back for a jump shot. His feet lift off of the ground and the ball floats up his body, a still, spinless globe in his loose hands, up his palm, his fingers, the open sky.

It misses everything – rim, backboard, net – and bounces loud into a stack of garbage cans. He hops on one foot and says, "Fuck that," under his breath, "Fucking fuck." Then looks at me quickly, to see if I heard.

"What?" I lie.

"We better get inside. It's early, sweetheart. One of the neighbors will start shouting."

I scurry for the ball.

"You're pretty good," he calls after me and for a moment I think he might add, *for a girl*, but he doesn't.

"Thanks, Dad."

"I bet you make the team."

"I'm going into fourth grade. We don't have teams yet, not real ones." "Oh, right. I mean, when you do."

We come into the kitchen. Gabby is seated at the counter. Teta's onions quiver the air over the stove as a vent fan tries to catch the smell and suck it out through the roof. Since it's morning, Dad disappears down the hall, to kneel at the foot of his bed.

Yesterday morning, after breakfast, Mom had made us wait and wait before we could go down to the beach. Gabby and I whined and complained and squirmed until Dad said, "Doctors and their thirty minutes be danged," and Gabby ran across the room and out the screen door, with Dad chuckling behind her along the short boardwalk. I hung back with Mom, folding towels and hanging them over the backs of chairs.

"Remember these towels when you come in," she said. "It took hours for the rug to dry, last time."

From where we sat, I could only see the top of Dad's head and the very tips of the waves.

"Mom?" I said a couple of times. Finally she looked up. "Should we be swimming?"

She grinned and shook a towel at me. "You ask me now? After all that drama?"

"That's not what I mean."

All week long we had watched the TV set in the corner, its screen flashing pictures of oil on the water. Of beaches spotted with globs like melted Hershey bars. Of miles of brightly colored floats trying to snake the waves clean, while the rust-orange ribbons snuck, swirling, around them. Maps of the Gulf coast looked like Crayola nightmares, with bright and scary colors just off shore, coming closer.

"Oh baby," she said, her hands smoothing the towels. "The oil isn't to the coast yet, swim while you can."

"But," I started, but she interrupted: "If I tell you not to worry, will you listen?"

"I can't help it."

Her hand stretched out, slow as time, to smooth the kinks in my hair. They bounced back under her fingers.

"I'll tell you what. I'll come down to the water in a little while, and I'll wade out past you, and spread out my arms to skim all of the oil back to sea."

"But if you do, the waves will bring more," I said, laughing.

"Then I'll huff and I'll puff, and I'll blow it back like clouds," she said, blowing on my face. Her breath smelled clean, too clean, metallic and antiseptic from within the folds of her head covering. "I'll blow it to the north and south of you and Gabby and your Dad, so you can have a little more sun, a little more playtime."

I laughed again and crawled into her lap, just for a moment, before sprinting down to the surf.

Now, the next day, at the kitchen counter, Gabby's back is to me. Her hair is brassy and brittle from the sun, still flecked with sand. I wonder why no one has tried to brush it out. Her chin is propped on the wooden counter, her arms hanging loose, her legs zig zags – as though someone set her down and, without arms to wrap her, she unraveled, waiting to be gathered together again.

Teta pinches saffron and salt through the air over the stove.

"We should do something fun today," she says, watching so the onions don't burn. "We can do whatever you want."

"What should we do?" Gabby asks.

"I think it would be a good idea if we went swimming. Would you like that?"

Gabby pushes at a knot in the counter that I never noticed before. She is going into first grade. She is so small.

"But Teta, didn't you hear?" she asks. "Our mother drowned at the beach."

"That's not the same thing," she said, her words sizzling the skillet. "She wasn't swimming."

I don't understand.

"She had no business going in the water, child, not at ten milligrams of Ativan a day. She could barely move her arms." Teta doesn't turn to look at us. Nothing moves on her, but the hand that stirs the spoon. "Good Lord, baby, your mother had a cancer. Didn't you know?"

I didn't.

"Fuck that," I say under my breath, so nobody can hear me but me. I put my arm around Gabby, my sweat cooling on my shoulders, mixing with the salt smell of the kitchen. I whisper in her ear, "Unfuck that."

Gabby looks at me with little big eyes, then hops down and runs up the hall. I follow after her to dig into my suitcase for a brush, then into her room to sit beside her on the bed. I brush her hair, then help her on with her shoes. As she is struggling with the knot, the loop and roll around her thumb, I lean against her, silently measuring my arm against hers. Anyone can see that mine is much longer, maybe even long enough to spread out north and south, to make a space of sun for her to play, yesterday forgotten like clouds.

i. racing the schoolyard

HE GREW UP with Lil, but never thought twice about her being a girl until the first time he saw her run. Not just run, but run fast – with a funny way of bringing her knees high at each step, holding her elbows in close, fists swinging like pistons.

He was in 5th grade; she was in 7th. He heard whispering in the school hallways before she did.

"Who do they say it was?" she asked. He tried to escape into the boy's bathroom but she followed him in.

"Nobody."

"You're a bad liar, Patete. How could it be nobody?" She was the first to call him Patete. It was French for little, she said, and she would stop when he was big enough to make her. Now everyone called him that.

So he told her what he'd heard: that it was Eric and Superchicken, two shooting guards from the JV. They said it was all her idea, that she drank until she saw stars and they had her at the paper-recycling warehouse, on a pile of porn and crosswords. Lil was so angry that she marched into 9th grade Geometry and called both of them to follow her outside.

"You want another go?" laughed Eric, and the class laughed with him. But the teacher, his bald head and mustache swelling, shouted until she closed the door.

She waited in the hall. When the bell rang, the whole class followed them out the double exit doors, into a parking lot frozen between an aluminum sky and claustrophobic concrete, and the smells of diesel and winter leaves. Lil and the boys walked ahead, like tall somebodies the others would never be.

"To the stop sign and back," she said.

Under his sweatshirt, Superchicken flexed his thin biceps. Behind him, Eric shuffled and blew into cupped hands.

"C'mon Lil, it's cold. Let's just go inside," Eric said.

"You talk like a man, why don't you show it?"

"I'm not cold," said Superchicken. "Anybody hear me say I'm cold?"

"Well I am," said Eric. "So let's do it or don't."

"One on one?" somebody asked, but Lil shook her head.

"Together. Like they say happened down at the recycling."

The boys laughed, then looked at her and thought better. Superchicken drew an invisible line with his foot.

"Ladies first, Lil."

"Don't you call me Lil."

Nobody said anything. After a few seconds, Patete said, quietly, "But Lil, that's your name."

"Shut up, Patete."

They started on a three count and when they reached the far stop sign, Lil was ahead by two strides. She was running harder than Patete had ever seen anyone run. Her feet blurred the ground and she bit at the air, her eyes swollen from crying, her light skin flushing, her legs as long as strings. But when they turned, the soles of her shoes slipped on loose ice and she went down, both hands splayed wide. The boys cornered expertly behind her and sprinted back toward the start.

Lil came up, her mouth a violent gash, her breath hot white. The huddled group backed away to clear a finish line just before Superchicken broke it, Eric neck and neck with him but Lil four steps back. She stood off to one side, her chest heaving, wiping long loops of spit from her mouth as Eric and Superchicken grinned around, pushing their way through the silent crowd to the rack where their Huffys were chained, then disappeared across the parking lot.

Patete followed Lil to the edge of the schoolyard, to a high metal fence – eight-foot tall corrugated sheets of tin laced together with baling wire. She pushed at one of the wide panels, scraping it against the cold dirt until she could squeeze through. A few seconds later, she swung it open again and looked out.

"What do you want, Patete?"

"Is it true?"

"Does it matter?"

"Okay."

She's a girl and girls don't bite, Patete had heard, not unless you ask them to. He was afraid she might take a swing at him just for thinking that.

"You remember when we used to play in the creek, all last summer?"

He nodded, slowly blinking, thinking of sun and shade.

"And after, we would eat melons we stole from the community garden? To see who could spit seeds the furthest."

"I never did that."

"You don't remember?"

"That wasn't me. That must have been someone else."

The tall fence panels spread in ripples left and right from where Patete stood, the metal clanging lightly under his knuckles.

"Maybe so," she said.

ii. summer swim

THE SUMMER BEFORE, on the last day of fourth grade, Patete had helped the man who lived with his mother – a man he had never called Dad – to carry tools down the street to Lil's house. He worked the loading docks at Home Depot; when tin sheets got bent, he would buy them off the manager for two dollars each, cash only, then hammer them straight and build fences all over the neighborhood.

Lil's mother said it wasn't safe for kids to play with so many sharp edges around, so she sent Lil and Patete to the creek. They made the long walk along the tracks, balancing on the rails and telling jokes, throwing dirt clods to burst, like dusty stars, on the clanging boxcars. They stole cardboard boxes from the recycling plant and rolled them down a steep embankment where the creek was knee-deep and brown. She ducked into the bushes to change into a bathing suit, while Patete watched flat-footed beetles walking on the creek's surface, shifting against the current, holding steady, gulping air. When Lil came out, they jumped from the box tops to splash in the water, over and over, until the boxes wet through and collapsed under them.

They went to the creek every day that summer – even after the fence was finished, even after the man left Patete's mother to move in with Lil's mother, even as Lil went deeper into the bushes to change.

On the day before school started, walking back from the creek, Patete saw wet triangles showing through Lil's clothes. She saw him looking and hit him in the chest, hard. He sat down, trying not to cry, then followed her at a distance, his hands bouncing against his thighs. When he reached her house, the high fence, Lil was waiting for him. She held a panel open, and through it Patete could see the grass tall against the house, so tall that only the roof was visible.

"He never mowed our yard either," he said. "I had to do it."

"I could mow it if I wanted."

"I hate mowing. It's boring."

"You're boring, and you can't come in."

Patete's face fell. "What? Why not?"

"He's here." She watched the house like it was watching her back. "You know, he gets Mom's pills from Mexico, cheaper than she can at the Bi-Lo. And she says he has needs, too."

Patete thought about standing in the school locker room, surrounded by boys who had hair showing on their arms and chests and between their legs. He never wanted to take his shirt off in the locker room, or in front of his mother, or anywhere except at the creek with Lil. And now, maybe not even there, not anymore.

"Anyway, he has a car. He lets me drive it sometimes."

"You're not old enough to drive," he said.

"So?"

"Okay, Lil." He kicked at the fence, his tennis shoes flicking dirt on his shirt. "Want to go to the creek after school tomorrow?"

"Soon it'll be too cold to swim. I don't want to catch sick."

"We don't have to swim. We could throw rocks, or tell jokes," Patete said. "I know some new ones."

"You know shit," she said.

All that fall, kudzu spilled over embankments and the sparrows that dotted the neighborhood flew only at night.

Patete saw Lil most days, getting in and out of cars in the high school parking lot. But she was too far away for him to hear her voice – only her laugh came bouncing back toward him, spinning the earth faster with each bounce, so he felt he was sprinting, out of breath, just to keep from falling. And he could not guess what was coming, beyond the weather and smells of exhaust and coal ash and fish frys, or what he would do, or what she would say.

iii. dinner time!

THE DAY before Thanksgiving, a police dispatcher chuckled at reports of a white man standing in the middle of Rossville Avenue, swinging a shotgun at the sky. When the patrol cars angled to a stop, their hands on sidearms, the man shouted that he was tired of the damn ducks skimming his rooftop, and wanted some dinner. The shotgun popped at his shoulder, echoing off the buildings around. Neighbors glanced at the windows, then went back to television.

But one duck jerked sideways, as if lassoed by an airy thread. It fell in a somersault, suddenly heavy, toward the ground before catching the air. Its wings beat furiously. The band on its neck dripped as it jittered over three, four blocks before tumbling hard into the short, grassy yards between two rows of identical houses.

From his window, Patete saw the duck land, green and white and brown and red into the grass. It stood on stick legs, one eye covered in dirt, its head looping a circle with each step, dragging its wing.

As he watched, a front door opened across the street and Mrs. Garcelle came out, holding a foot-long serrated bread knife. Patete knew her as a girthy woman, always on her front porch, and it seemed strange to see her, out in the yard, in her house dress. Looking up, she saw him watching and held one finger to her mouth, shhhh, but farther down the street another door opened and another woman came out, shouldering bra straps into place, a rolling pin in her hand. The duck started waddling fast, arching one wing high, the other loose and useless. More doors opened. Men and women stalked the short walkways.

Patete sat at his window for a long time, for hours after dinner had been cooked and the dishes put away, waiting for morning to flood the world.

iv. a mother's errand

HIS MOTHER leaned back against the refrigerator door, a hazy ring of fingerprints and magnets over her head. Patete poked his head around the corner, grinning at her, his mouth making an unsteady butterfly shape.

"I know what's in the fridge, Patete," she said. "Why didn't you clean it up? Is it milk?"

He nodded, still standing in the doorway.

"I don't want to know what happened," she said. "It doesn't matter why you stop being a child, Patete, or where, or even how. Only that it happens, and happens soon."

On the floor beside her was a plate of half-eaten macaroni, smeared with cheese powder, crusting over. Patete could smell its stink from the doorway. She was still wearing the brown uniform, unbuttoned over her undershirt; the security guard patch gaped like a flap of skin above her low breasts.

"Come sit with me, honey."

"I already ate. I had cereal."

"With milk. Don't I know it."

It was Saturday morning, the day after Lil's race. Patete wanted to tell her about Lil all but beating two boys, but he knew better; when his mom came from work, she was headed to bed.

She patted the hard linoleum and he sat, tucking his head under her arm. He leaned into her, rising and falling on her breathing.

"You know I'm proud of you baby. You let yourself in and lock up. You look after yourself all night. But it's not enough, and I'm trying, but I just can't make do."

"I know," he said, not understanding.

She held her breath, half in half out, until he bounced his head on her chest and she exhaled, words rushing out of her mouth. "They say God is outside of time and place, Patete, so maybe there are things he can't remember. But I remember everything. And every time I pass that house I hate God like I hate him, and her, and even Lil, for stealing away the little bit of ease I'd gathered." She wiped her face. "I hate everything that won't stop the world turning long enough for me to jump clear."

Patete stared at her until she said, "No, baby, I don't really hate Lil. Not anymore."

He kissed her cheek and said, "Go to bed, Mom. I'll go to the park."

"Maybe could you walk past her house, on the way? Just one time."

She touched his elbow as she said it. Every Saturday, the same question – just one time past Lil's driveway, to see if that old blue Honda was parked there. Maybe slip into the side yard, push at the fence panels, peek through. The man had caught Patete once, bending him across his knee like a father. But Patete knew that, when he came home, her expression would be the same whether the Honda was there or not. Her bubble of strength would vanish without any noise at all, not even a popping sound, and there would be nothing for him to do but go into his room to play, and pray for her to stop crying, but she wouldn't, and wouldn't.

"I should be strong," she said; but he interrupted her:

"I will."

"You're my good boy," she said thickly. "My man of the house."

As soon as he was outside, however, Patete turned in the opposite direction. The street was sunny and warm, without any of the ice of the day before. Neighbors sat on porches, watching flickering televisions through open windows; children in diapers played with dogs on yard chains. Patete stood in line at the 7-Eleven for a bag of Skittles, then went to the park. He sat on metal bleachers, lining up the round-flat candy on the empty bench, row by row by color.

Groups of older kids were already playing pick-up, at each end of the outdoor court. They collided under netless rims, guessing where each other was going to be, throwing arms wide, gripping jerseys. The ball skipped low on the ground between them, hand to hand. Patete watched, thinking he would never be so long-armed, so teenaged, so sure of where his feet hit the ground.

Superchicken was there, shorter and pushing harder than the others, pointing and shouting, one hand in the air, the other loose and kinetic at his side. The ball stammered, started one way, got fearless, stopped; started another way, struck, marked time, started again; then seemed to have found a direction, struck again, got stuck.

Then Lil appeared, stepping out of the blue Honda before it roared toward home. Patete crouched in the bleachers, staring at her as she laughed and clapped, not at all the same person she had been the day before. She ignored Superchicken as he dribbled close to her, bringing the ball up court, then suddenly turned and pretended to throw it at her. Lil shrugged her shoulders in a mock reflex, not even taking her hands out of her pockets. They laughed, together, the sound of it rolling across the blacktop, across the grass, slowing to a stop at Patete's feet.

He peered out from behind the bleachers. Nobody was looking, so, pocketing the candy, he hurried across the open field, his face turned away from the court. From behind him, dribbling came in an unpredictable rhythm, then silence, a backboard shaking. He wondered exactly what was happening; the whole world seemed to be at his back, just out of sight, focused and sharp, magnetic. Lil laughed again, and he knew that he had missed something that meant something to her. He wondered how many laughs he had missed in the months that had passed since they went swimming in the creek, and he felt the first great pain of his life.

At the long rack of bicycles, all neatly rowed, all unchained, he found Superchicken's bike – an old Huffy, spray painted purple, a bell twisted onto the spokes with a paperclip. He looked backward. Superchicken was pretending to slap Lil's face. She slapped back at him and he clapped his hands together, the sound resonant and full, pretending to stagger backward.

"If my fists and feet were strong, I could hit and run," Patete whispered to himself, imagining attacking like a bird out of the bushes, inhuman and brutal. "Then Lil would see me with a missing tooth, or a blacker eye. She would say, What were you thinking Patete? And I would say, Don't call me that."

Reaching, taking both handlebars, he pulled the purple Huffy out of the rack. The grips were cold in his hands. He looked up to see Lil staring at him, shaking her head, fast. From behind her, Superchicken was sprinting toward him.

"Run, Patete, now," Lil shouted over the sound of the wind already rushing in his ears.

v. kissing at the creek

PATETE STOOD, brushing his knees, watching circles spread in the muddy water. A car came barreling into the recycling lot, a hundred feet away. It was the blue Honda, with the driver's seat as far forward as it could go. Lil unlocked the doors. Patete ran around the car and opened the passenger door, into her candy-wrapper smell.

"Boy, you're in some trouble."

"I am?"

"You have to ask?" She cracked the window. "Quiet." But it was only a train on the tracks. "Don't you know what he's like? What were you thinking?"

"I thought maybe I'd sell it to Dom. I thought I could get some money, maybe buy something." He didn't say what he wanted to buy.

"Oh Patete," she said and shifted into drive, kicked at the accelerator. "How much did he give you?"

"Dom said if it was stolen, he would beat me silly. A stolen bike at his door means cops at his door. So I ran it into the creek."

The engine thunked through the gears and they cut up an alley. Bricks slid past, weaving close on either side, then dropped away as the car soared, without slowing, across oncoming traffic. She tried to cut the steering wheel, nearly made it, might have made it except for a UPS truck parked at the corner. Her fender clipped the truck's back tire, and it burst in thunder and rubber that flew like shrapnel, shattering the windshield into a web of grey-green cracks. The car fishtailed into the side of the truck and stopped dead. Patete had to crawl over the gearshift and out of Lil's door, after her.

"What the hell is that truck doing parked there, nine on a Saturday morning?

"You wrecked his car. What will he do when he sees it?"

"What? Who?" before she realized. "Don't worry, Patete," she said softly. "Maybe I can talk to him, too. Maybe I can fix everything."

She pulled at his arm, tugging him around the side of the building and Patete saw that they were standing in the schoolyard. The high, metal fence was ten steps away. She pushed through it; he pushed through after her.

His arm was bleeding through his sweatshirt. He wished that she would notice, come and roll up the sleeve, but she was standing with her back to him, facing the house. Around her, the grass was tall on every side. The curling leaves, winter thin, waved in the morning air.

"I should go and tell him about his car," she said. "We should go around the house and come in the front door. Make something up."

But instead, she took his hand and led him deeper into the grass. When they could almost see the windows, but not quite, she stopped and was very still.

"Remember last summer, Patete, when we used to go swimming in the creek? I never told anybody about that."

"Why not?"

The grass was taller than Patete. He felt its razor edges on every side, except where Lil's body parted it, in front of him. He felt like he had been swallowed by the fence, the grass, the yard.

"How old are you, Patete?"

"I'm still eleven."

"That means I'm still thirteen. A lot can happen in a few months, Patete. Things that make you a different person."

"You don't seem different to me."

She might have touched his hand; he wasn't sure. Around them, the wrinkled leaves on the stalks rippled together, like fragile fingers reaching for something primitive and certain.

"Maybe some things never change," she said. She turned to face him. He was so close to her mouth that clouds of her breath wrapped his neck. "Look at me, Patete. When you look at me, I don't seem so different to me, either."

She came closer, blinking slowly, her eyes crossing slightly, as if she were hunting a reflection in his wet eyes. When they met, he closed his mouth into hers, not knowing how, only knowing why, and breathed her in as deep as he could.

Afterward, he said, "That's all there is to it?"

"That's all there is," she said. And they sat in the tall grass, choosing candy out of his palm, biting the sugar shell away from the sour centers.

vi. lock and cock it.

IT WAS AFTER NOON when Patete's mother woke to the sound of the doorbell. It rang over and over, fast, echoing itself. Balled hands pounded the door.

She got up slowly from the kitchen floor, felt her way through the house in the curtained dark, not turning lights on as she went. The front door was outlined in daylight; two shadow feet scuffed erratically on the boards of the porch.

"Momma, Mom, please just turn the knob, quick," she heard through the door. She pressed her eye to the view hole.

"Patete, what have you done now?" she called. His face filled the fisheye lens, streaked with tears. Behind him, a car she had never seen before pulled short at the edge of the yard. Its passenger door opened, a boy already running out of it, his face shining with rage, his arms stiffening.

Patete turned, saw, threw himself against the door once again, knowing it wouldn't open. His mouth gaped against the unyielding wood.

"No, Mom. Please."

The dead bolt tripped closed beneath her fingers, the steel filling the lock. As she watched through the glass, her son turned to face the yard. Other boys poured out of the car, forming a half circle, stomping, laughing.

"Someday you'll be a man," his mother called through the wood. "Be strong, Patete. Kick his ass."

Superchicken tore off his sweatshirt as he reached the steps, not slowing. Patete stepped out from beneath the shaded porch to meet him, his fists lifted small.

IT WAS STILL RAINING – evening and morning, the third day. Hal was chewing the knotted hood-string of his sweatshirt, fraying the braid between his teeth as the waitress held a pot of coffee over Guthrie's head, like a threat.

Guthrie sat without moving, big as the whole booth. His triple-XL jean jacket was still not quite dry.

"You should think twice about that, lady," Hal said. "You might be surprised, I've seen him move fast before."

She pretended to be joking and topped off Guthrie's cup. He creased three packets of Domino sugar under his big thumbnail, tore them into his mug, and ordered another apple turnover.

"It's none of my business, mister," she said, her mouth wound in taut disapproval. "But if you start every day like this, you're due a heart attack."

He pointed a spoon at her. "If you're calling me fat, just out and say it."

"I didn't say fat."

"Nobody said fat, Guthrie."

"Well, we're all saying it now," he said.

"I didn't mean anything," the waitress said. "I could stand to lose a few pounds, myself."

"Your words, lady. Not mine," Guthrie muttered into the swirling mug.

She stepped backward and put the pot on the counter, out of her own reach. "I'm not sure what that means, mister, but I'm sure I don't like it."

Guthrie took a bite and chewed slowly. "It means, not only do you serve shit at this diner but damned if you don't talk it too."

Hal sighed. "Guthrie, what'd you have to say that for?"

"I'd like you to leave," she said, her eyes blackening.

"You can't kick us out."

"What do you mean, us? What did I do?" asked Hal, glancing at the iron clouds, at the sheeting rain.

"We're paying customers, lady."

"So pay right now. Both of you."

Guthrie was already sliding out of the booth, headed toward the register, twisting his broad mechanic's hand into the pocket of his Levis. He paid for both breakfasts then walked, slow, back to the table, his huge bald head floating over the booths like a paraded idol, to leave a fifty dollar tip under the ashtray. That's Guthrie's way – always setting things straight, but only after he breaks them.

THE LAST regular job Guthrie had, he was night watchman at the Marriott parking garage. He liked walking the quiet rows of cars, watching over things that he didn't own, that he didn't really worry about. He was in the best shape of his life then, slim and lanky; late nights he would race the elevator up and down the stairs, for fun. His hair was buzzed short to hide where he was balding, so he looked ex-Military, or like a state trooper, only softer around the eyes. He didn't look like what he was – a man out of Silverdale early for good behavior.

He lost that job because the manager's daughter got him fired. One night, after a binge down at the brewery, she parked in the handicapped space beside Guthrie's attendant booth, looked him up and down, and tossed him the keys. Then she crawled into the back seat and took off all her clothes.

Guthrie peered in through the window. She looked up at him, her face pale under his own reflection, and all he could see was trouble.

So he dropped the keys on the front seat, locked the doors and walked away as she pressed, furious, against the window.

Before she woke the next morning, one of the kids who worked the breakfast bar walked past – angry at his job, at the hotel, at a world that would allow morning and night to orbit just so he could serve limp bacon and toast to travelers. He saw a car in the handicapped parking space without a hang-tag on the mirror and, hungry for justice, took out his keys to scratch up the car's paint job. But lo and behold, a naked woman was in the back seat, streaks of eyeliner dried down her face. A face he recognized.

She woke up to the chirp of her cell phone and a text message photo of herself, passed out, ass-up to the world. Tugged her clothes on and marched inside, telling her daddy that it was all Guthrie's fault, his name angry spit on her lips. So the manager called Guthrie's house and woke him up just to threaten him, to say don't bother ever coming back.

Guthrie waited a few days, and then hung around the attendant's station after dark. The kid from the breakfast bar had been promoted to night watch, and came along proudly shaking Guthrie's old key ring in his pocket, talking on the cell phone. He never saw Guthrie rising out of a shadow to wrap both hands around his collar, pull him into the dark space between two cars.

He pinned the boy to the pavement with his knees and untwisted a coat hanger from his pocket, jimmied one of the car doors open. The kid twisted and kicked, struck out, but Guthrie carefully placed the boy's hand, with the phone clenched in it, over the hinge of the open car door and pushed it closed, in no hurry. Crushing until he felt plastic and glass and bone give way.

"Let this be a lesson," Guthrie said.

He walked down the garage ramp just as the manager's daughter turned in. Knocked on her window. She said that she wouldn't get him his job back, but Guthrie took the folded coat hanger out of his pocket. She cringed backward in the seat, afraid, but Guthrie only slid his hand, slow, easy, along the window seal and showed her how to pop a door lock.

She laughed and hit him, playful, across his chest. He let her choose a few luxury sedans in the garage, showed her how to disable an alarm and hotwire an engine. He even let her drive them around the deck, and park them in different places than their owners left them. But he wouldn't let her take them out into the street. He didn't want her to get in real trouble, he told Hal later. He just hated to leave her feeling ugly.

STEPPING OUT of the diner, Hal pulled the sleeves of his sweatshirt down over his hands, bunching them in his grip. He was tall and very thin, unshaven beneath a dirty baseball cap, the whiskers thickest on his upper lip, his mouth held sideways, like he had just forgotten what he was going to say, or like he was going to be sick.

The rain felt cold on his unshowered skin as he ran with short steps, careful not to fall, and slipped into the back seat of Guthrie's old Mercedes.

Guthrie had bought the car on auction and dropped a modified Chevrolet engine into it himself, with Hal passing him the wrenches. Hal had never understood the appeal – the floorboards rusting through under the mats, the seat leather cut and torn all over. Children in Guthrie's apartment building had torn the Mercedes symbol off the hood, and Hal often said that, without that chrome peace sign, it looked like a clown car.

Guthrie came into the lot, blinking in the rain, pulling an enormous stocking cap down to the collar of a wrinkled camouflage poncho. Hal watched him come closer, thinking – good thing the car has room for all three of us; if push comes to shove and the cops show up, or alarms sound, or word somehow gets out, we can park somewhere hidden and quiet, and have room to stretch out and sleep for a couple days.

IN THE SATURDAY quiet of the Southside, the Seventh Day Adventists' prerecorded bells, tinny and loud, chastised anyone trying to ignore their Sabbath. They woke Hal in time to bundle his sister Margaret into scarves and blankets, wrap her securely into the rusty electric wheelchair and push her next door to Miss Bentley's apartment. Margaret, never talking but never quite quiet, always in the background of family portraits, of his childhood, of his mind.

After their mother died, Hal had moved back into her house, thinking that despite its creaks and drafty walls and Margaret, it was better than no house at all. But it only took a few weeks before the house seemed to start coming apart around him – board by board, nail by nail, each one pulled out of place and sucked along the long hallway into the black hole of Margaret's room.

So he started wheeling her to Miss Bentley's and spending weekends with Guthrie. He would unload her in Miss Bentley's spare bedroom and double-check the cabinets for diabetes and reflux and gas medicines, adult diapers and waterproof ointments and vitamin supplements, making a list of what to buy at the Wal-Mart. Life extended another week by the welfare check, by small comforts packed into blue plastic shopping bags.

Guthrie took him in gladly, saying that Hal had earned any bit of fun they could hustle here and there. Sometimes, at bowling or a bar, people would make comments and implications. One time, at the Fire Hall, one of the firemen called him faggot. Hal came at him, fists clenched, but Guthrie stepped in between with a serious smile, telling how Hal sets a fork, knife and spoon before Margaret at every meal, even if there is only soup to eat. How he bathes her, and takes her on the bus to the hospital twice a month.

"That should tell you something about what makes a man," Guthrie said. "Who wouldn't be lucky to have such a brother?"

Hal would sit, listening to them talk about him, waiting to hear something that would tell him what to think of himself. Hoping to catch a clue, a depth of insight, a hint of a life cracking over the horizon – almost anything would do, so long as it was big enough to make sense of everything. But it never came. They would go back to Guthrie's apartment to sit and watch ESPN for hours on end; Hal would sit at the far end of the couch, out of reach, but sneaking glances at Guthrie.

THE MERCEDES turned out of the diner, toward downtown. Three miles on the map, Main Street ran in a straight line from one T-end to the other, from warehouses surrounded by public housing to warehouses that backed onto the river. Dead in the middle were four blocks of refurbished lofts and studios and restaurants, art galleries and an artisan butcher – a pocket microhood, a promise to turn the clock simultaneously forward and backward.

Windows in these four blocks were cluttered with posters for The Main Street Fall Festival. Local crafts, beers and bratwurst, kiddie carnival rides. A paper banner hung in wet scraps, the words World Famous in Chattanooga dripping into potholes, into the muddied reflections of storefronts.

The car pulled up to the sidewalk, out back of the Fire Hall. Dixson was standing on the sidewalk, smoking.

"Guthrie, I have a confession to make," he said, sitting into the front seat and patting his pockets for a dry cigarette. "I've got the jitters."

"Me too," said Hal.

"How long has it been, Guthrie? Since you pulled a gun on a crowd of people and shouted: Good people of Chattanooga, touch the ceiling."

"Not long enough. And I don't expect to tonight. No point shouting to an empty building."

Dixson's face looked pale and his hands were shaking, just like always. He was a slight man with long sideburns, always fidgeting and shifting in his skin, up late and up early, drinking all night, then spending his days on a tall stool in the Fire Hall's ready room, scrubbing mops in the deep sink, an unlit cigarette in his fingers, his thin cheeks puffing with effort.

A pee-wee Ferris wheel, no more than twenty feet tall, spun by outside the window.

"Where are all the people? There were supposed to be hundreds, thousands," Dixson said. "They were all supposed to be buying beer and groceries, filling the cash registers."

"Too late to call it off now," said Guthrie.

They stopped at a red light.

"What will you do with your share?" Dixson asked.

"I don't know how much we'll get, so how can I know how I'll spend it?"

"No matter how much it is, I'm headed for Tunica. Turn a bit into a bundle. I found a blackjack Web site written by a math genius, that tells you when to double down, when to stand."

"That's counting cards," Hal said. "Like in that movie, with the retard."

"You, of all people, should not use that word."

"Careful," said Guthrie, his eyes widening and slitting.

"Anyway, it's not counting cards," Dixson said quickly, changing the subject. "It's playing the overlay. When God, or luck, or whatever smiles on you. Good cards in your hand, real money on the table, odds on your side."

He cracked the window to let the smoke out, and rain flicked through to the back seat. Hal didn't mind; it felt light and fresh and cool on his face.

"I'm no gambler," Guthrie said.

"Won't gamble, or can't? I heard you're banned at every table from St. Louis to Cherokee."

"Not won't. Not can't. Don't."

"That was a long time ago, Dixson," Hal cut in. "I figure they'd take him back now, if he wanted."

They stopped at an empty park playground to piss through the fence. Raindrops beaded on the fence links; patches of uncut grass bent calisthenic in the wind. They drove back along Main, where stores were cutting down the banners and locking up early. In the houses surrounding, yellow living room lights were warm, shut tight against the weather. Hal thought of Margaret, that it was nearly time for her dinner, and was glad to be in the car.

"What'll you spend your money on, Hal?" Dixson asked over the seat, making nice. But Guthrie interrupted: "I guess we'll all spend it on whatever we worry about."

Hal thought, I guess he's right.

HE KNEW Guthrie planned to get the stomach staple with his share, and he couldn't help feeling it was his fault. It seemed wrong to him that so much ache, a need for scalpels and stitches, should come from the simple joys of butter and sugar.

During the long weekdays alone in the house with Margaret, living by television, Hal had found cable channel cooking and started preparing elaborate meals for his sister. He would weigh every ingredient, following the chef on the small screen religiously. Soon he was stealing cookbooks from the public library, experimenting with stocks and syrups, teaching himself to julienne and chiffonade. Then he would scrape the plate into a blender, liquefying everything for her to drink it through a washable plastic straw.

Morning and night, morning and night, tipping the grey mix to her gaping birdling mouth, her garbage disposal mouth. Hal tried to make it into a way to care about caring for her, but no matter how much he spiced and battered and basted, loaded and unloaded the sink, iced the oven blisters on his fingers and forearms, she slurped the same. He tried to resist – to hate hate, to love – but she simply she took it all, and wanted more.

So he started doubling each recipe and taking the second plate to Guthrie. Carefully wrapping dishes in cling film, carefully wrapping Margaret in blankets and pushing her chair with its dead battery down the street to Guthrie's apartment at the old Days Inn. Before long, Guthrie knew to open the door before Hal even knocked, coming outside to sit on the curb, eating his dinner between where Hal sat silent and Margaret sat moaning.

In less than one year, Guthrie gained nearly a hundred pounds. The next year, seventy more. It was as if Hal's extra servings touched off something in him, and he found himself getting up after midnight to visit drive-thrus. On the weekends when Hal slept on his couch, they went to the grocery together and came out carrying bags peaked with meats and breads, fresh herbs and new flavors, cases of beer paid for by hawking Margaret's food stamps. Guthrie, burly and red-faced, already grinning, sat onto the couch and didn't stand up until the next day. Hal was happy cooking in the kitchen, listening to the TV from the living room. Knowing that someone else would be turning Margaret in her bed, wiping her with the washcloth, tipping meals into the whirling tooth of the blender, threading the straw between her colorless lips.

Guthrie sometimes brought girls home, and Hal would curl in his bedroll on the couch, wondering what would happen if he got caught peeking in the bedroom door. One time, Guthrie went for beer and came back with a case under each arm and two girls he had picked up at the bowling alley. Hal was already asleep in his bedroll when they burst into the apartment.

"Want some dessert?" Guthrie called, sitting on the couch. He bent forward, pulling off his shoes and socks. The skin of his ankles showed compression lines from the socks' elastic, and the black hairs were flattened. He pulled the girl he had chosen for himself into his big lap; the other took Hal by the arm and led him to the bedroom.

"But this isn't my bed," Hal said, and the girl laughed. She was short, the top of her head at Hal's shoulders, and dressed for a night out. Her sequined shirt was too tight across the hips and the tumble of stomach sweated through the cotton. Her big thighs chafed in the skirt, and her calves ran straight down into her feet, making folds over the tops of her bowling shoes.

"I didn't steal these shoes, I'm in a bowling league," she said. "Plus they're good for my plantar fasciitis.

Her thick, tightly curled hair smelled like plastic fruit. It made Hal feel young and jumpy to sit beside her on the unmade bed.

"When I dressed nice today, I knew there was a reason. That tonight was going to be special." She sat closer, one hand flat on the bed.

"I don't know," said Hal.

"I'll do you right, Henry. It is Henry, right?"

Hal shrugged.

"Sweet Henry," she said, her hand on his. "Only, you have to promise not to look too close. I'm not so pretty naked."

Her arms shook out of the shimmering top, her hair dropping like hushed sunshine through her fingers.

"I think you're very pretty," he said. "It's not that."

"Oh, then. You don't have to worry about the other. I don't bleed, on account I'm heavy. You don't have anything to worry about."

Hal closed his eyes, pretending. Afterward, the girl dressed and left immediately, with her friend and one of the cases of beer. Hal lay on the living room floor, watching TV, as Guthrie made loud sleeping noises from the couch – less snoring than a deep, painful, hard work of breathing, more gasp and groan than rest.

It reminded him of his mother's breathing, which had always been strained, even when he was very small. She would curl up next to his pillow and tell him stories about the Man in the Moon, the jolly face that smiled down proud on all he sees below. But for as long as he could remember, when Hal looked at the moon all he could see was Margaret's fat face, her moaning mouth, her eyes wide in horror and ununderstanding, stupid to the world's hurt, an idiot child forever confused and afraid.

The next morning, Hal took Guthrie to the Bi-Lo, to sit in the car with a pair of binoculars. He told Guthrie how Miss Bentley had been let go from her job as Assistant Manager a few months back, corporate downsizing. She had been angry ever since, and would rant for hours over detailed sketches of where they kept the cash box, of inventory timetables and bank runs.

Guthrie hesitated, until he thought of the Main Street Fall Festival, when cash registers would be bursting with tourist dollars. He said he liked the sound of a take big enough to get them through winter. Maybe even pay for something important.

WHEN HAL WOKE, they were parked at a gas pump. The hood was up, and through the gap Hal could see Guthrie bent over the engine, wearing the camouflage poncho, his hands moving expertly among the dip sticks and fuses.

Dixson slid back into the front seat, a box of longnecks in his lap.

"I bet he checks it every time he fills the tank. Like an old woman."

The car shook as Guthrie shut the hood. He pulled the car around to the back of the service station and locked it, then the three of them crossed Main Street, to Murphy Bros Tire & Auto.

Out front, the low building was hung with wide, lime green awnings. Earl Murphy met them inside the door. He looked out of place in his own clothes, his skin too wrinkled to be handsome any more, his jaw always working. He shook Guthrie's hand and led them into an office that was paneled in painted wood and hung with photographs of fireworks over the river.

A desk as wide as the room sat against one wall, and behind it was a tall man with thick, ringed fingers. Murph Murphy seemed much younger than his brother, but wore Walmart eyeglasses that made his eyes look rounder than they actually were, as if he were always straining to see; when he took them off them to wipe the lenses clean, his eyes sunk away in his face. He did not stand or shake hands.

"Jeremiah Guthrie," said Earl, "This is my brother Murph."

"Did he call you Jeremiah?" Murph asked.

"Hm," Guthrie said, and shook his head. "Just Guthrie."

Hal stepped forward, thinking Guthrie would introduce him. But no one moved or spoke, so he leaned back against the wall.

"How do you know my brother, Mr. Guthrie?"

"We've known each other a long time," said Earl. "Hell, everybody knows Guthrie."

"And I guess you two are his boys?"

Dixson said, around a cigarette, "Sure we are."

"Would you please not smoke inside? It's bad for business."

"I don't mind," said Dixson, crushing it out.

"Women from Cincinnati or Cleveland come to visit our fair city, you see, and they need their oil changed before the long trip home. They don't want to breathe smoke. You understand."

"I don't mind," Dixson said again.

"Mr. Guthrie," Murph said, hesitating, as if he weren't quite sure of how to pronounce the name. "My brother told me your plan, but I'm not sure that you're the right man for the job."

"With respect, you don't have to be sure of anything. It's not your job." Guthrie stood in the center of the room, facing the desk, and Hal thought about all the muscle it must take to carry all that weight.

"So why'd you tell my brother? For the hell of it?"

"More or less," said Guthrie.

"More, or less?"

"It's not like that, Murph," Earl said, from the corner. "When someone buys a pistol out of the trunk of a car on the Southside, word gets to me. To you, I mean, but to me too. Like I said, I know Guthrie, so I thought maybe we can help."

"That's lucky."

"Sure it is," said Guthrie.

"It's more than lucky, Mr. Guthrie," Murph said. "Because the very store you're planning to rob is a place we've wanted to get inside for months."

"I don't remember having seen you in the bushes with binoculars," said Guthrie.

Murph chewed on the eraser end of a pencil, spitting bits of red rubber onto the carpet.

"But you see, Mr. Guthrie, the lock box of that store holds an envelope of papers that I want. If you break in tonight, there will be new locks, more patrols. So we have two choices. Either you call it off, or you help us out."

"Listen here. I don't mean disrespect, but I'm only here as a favor to your brother," Guthrie said.

"Save your favors. We'll give you five grand."

Guthrie stood up straighter. "Just for the papers? We keep any cash we find."

"That's not my business, so long as that envelope lands on this desk."

"See?" said Earl. "Wasn't that easy?"

"Sure it was. Why not."

"Why not," said Guthrie.

Hal couldn't help himself. "What's in the envelope?" he asked.

Guthrie spoke fast, for the first time. "He doesn't need to know, Mr. Murphy. We don't need to know. The way I see it, if I'm going to empty a man's cash drawer, I might as well pick up the mail on the way out. Without opening it."

Dixson pulled a cigarette out of the pack, remembered, stuffed it in his shirt pocket. It broke and tobacco scattered on the floor. He knelt, awkwardly, brushing the withered leaves into his palm.

"One more question, Mr. Guthrie. You'll forgive me for asking, but are you in shape to pull it off? I don't want you having a heart attack on the doorstep. What if you have to run for it?"

Guthrie put both of his hands behind his back. The fingers barely touched. The camouflage poncho flared, its oversized leaves and branches filling the space, surrounding the desk and walls and men. Damn, Hal thought, he must weigh nearly four hundred pounds. The storm beat on the roof, inches above their heads.

At last Murph said, "Okay. I guess, with a gun in your hands, you have options."

Down Main Street, Chattanooga Creek was spilling over its bridges. On East 3rd, a car was submerged to its windshield. Another was flipped onto its side, the current turning the tires and frothing the black underchassis. They drove slowly, watching the water rise like a high tide.

"My brother's house flooded once, in Missouri," Dixson said. "The river filled his house a foot deep. Water swelled up the floorboards and the sheetrock, until the walls crumbled away."

They stopped for Big Macs and Guthrie paid with his Visa card, calling it a business expense. Dixson asked the girl at the window why McDonalds doesn't serve beer with dinner, and she said she's looking at three good reasons. They all laughed and she laughed too. She had a dusky laugh that ended in a hoarse cough. A radio sound.

In the Bi-Lo parking lot, they sat eating burgers and digging in the cardboard case until the beers were gone. Then they drove across the street and parked at a hotel.

"How many?"

"Three."

"Any kids?"

"Just us."

"I don't like this place," Dixson whispered to Hal, too loud, the beer strong on his breath. "Look at that beard. I don't think he's an American." Hal moved away, hoping he wouldn't say it louder. Dixson faded outside, patting his pockets.

"Two double beds?"

Guthrie glanced at Hal and asked the man, "You have a rollaway?"

"Course. That's seventy-five, plus twenty for the rollaway."

"Thanks but no thanks."

"Hold on a minute," the man said. "Maybe you could have a room with two twins and the rollaway, for fifty-five."

Guthrie peeled out cash this time, not wanting to use his credit card just across the street from the Bi-Lo.

"What you think of all this rain?" the clerk asked.

"It's a goddamn shame, that's what I think," said Guthrie, then immediately said, "Sorry. I don't mean to be rude. It's just a shame."

They walked across the street to the grocery. Out behind the delivery alley, a flooded field was creeping close. Guthrie led them all of the way around the building, circling it once, then inside to pick up a case of High Life and some chips.

The aisles were empty except for a few employees in red vests stocking shelves. Through the wide windows, the silhouettes of cars passed now and again. At the check-out, Guthrie tapped Hal on the arm and pointed at the store manager.

He had a potbelly and a glossy haircut. His nose filled his face, fair hairs springing from it, over a small, mismatched grin. A wide necktie rested on his belly like a sketch of an arrow, pointing vaguely forward. He was a man who spent his life choosing not to be angry at angry customers, angry delivery men and stock boys, an angry wife and angry children. A life of hiring and scheduling, stocking shelves, rebudgeting. He walked leaning forward, slightly, following the doubtful arrow that hung down his chest, pointing where to go.

"How you boys this afternoon?" he asked over the noise of the conveyer belt. "Homes flooded? I hear hotels are filling up."

Hal pretended to look at the covers of the magazines until he couldn't stand it any longer.

"It never rains like this in New York City," he blurted.

"That right? You all from New York City?"

"Sure we are," Hal said.

Dixson shook his head, not looking up.

The manager looked from face to face. "I'm not from here, myself," he said. "Been here five years, although I hardly ever get out of the store. It's a big job, managing a grocery, bigger than people think. You boys get bottled water? The news says don't drink from the tap." Guthrie held up the beer and the manager, always ready to please, said, "Even better. Leave the water for the locals."

Back in the hotel room, with their shoes piled in a comfortable mess, Dixson and Guthrie stretched out on the twin beds, drinking and watching TV, while Hal unfolded the rollaway. After an hour, Dixson lurched to the bathroom and passed out with his cheek against the toilet seat.

Guthrie said, "I think maybe you shouldn't have said so much to that manager man."

"He won't remember, by tomorrow."

"He thinks we're out of towners, Hal. We'll come to mind for sure."

"He'll have plenty of other things to think about. He won't remember us at all."

"Maybe. If we're lucky."

"And if he does, we can pay him a visit. Make him forget."

"No, Hal. I don't want any of that sort of thing."

"Then what did you get guns for?"

"I said I got guns, I didn't say I got ammo," Guthrie said. "There's a world of difference, Hal, between blocking a punch and pulling a trigger."

Hal didn't like this. He thought of stories he had heard about Guthrie, young and tall and strong. He thought about the plastic bag under Guthrie's pillow, the pistols inside of it, the perfectly round barrels, the grips for holding on tight. And he realized that he had been thinking about holding a pistol in his hand for weeks. Because then, getting what he wanted would be as simple as taking it.

"New York City, what the hell," Guthrie laughed without really laughing. "What were you thinking, Hal?"

"I don't know," he said, and before he had time to think, added, "Maybe we could go there."

Guthrie tried to stand, unsuccessfully, and Hal thought how much a fat man looks like a baby. He wondered how much money they would have to find in the store's lockbox to pay for two plane tickets, instead of one. Guthrie could use his share for his operation, and Hal could split his share down the middle: two tickets to New York, or even farther away. Far away enough for Guthrie to recover, to heal.

This life shouldn't be full of hope, Hal thought. It shouldn't be a life of waiting and wanting. I don't know what this want means, and I don't care, either. I won't question or poke or prod it, because at least I know what I want.

And he thought that right now, with Dixson unconscious and unhearing on the bathroom floor, he might tell Guthrie everything he wanted. He built up breath in his lungs.

"How drunk are you, Guthrie?"

"Pretty drunk, I guess."

"If I say something, you think you'll remember?"

"Sure as sober, Hal. Don't say anything you can't unsay." Guthrie rolled over so he was facing out the horizontal slash of the window. "Why don't we talk about the money, instead?" he said quietly, looking out the window. "I can get my staple, and Margaret can have her operation, too. If there's only enough for one, if we have to choose, we'll give it to her."

Hal had never said anything about an operation. There was no surgery, no medicine that could help her.

"But don't you think we'll have to leave town?" Hal said, his voice unsteady.

"Why would we leave?"

"Just to get out and lay low. Even if only for a little while."

"You're not talking sense, Hal." Guthrie's voice ricocheted around the room, and he nodded at its echo. "There's something rooted in you, and me, and Dixson, too. Something twisted into us from the ground up, I don't know if we were born with it, or if it's in the water, or what. But we're not going anywhere, none of us. You might try to claw free, but if you do, then the very ground around you will shift and shudder, so slow at first you can't feel it. But then the axis tilts, and you slip and slide right back home."

"Wait, what did you say?" Hal said, trying to sit upright, his cheek sticking to the rollaway's thin pillow.

"Just try to pack up and leave, Hal. You'll find I'm right."

"You said you, and me, and Dixson," Hal said, a wet hot core of anger flooding his veins, his marrow. "You take it back. He's nothing like you and me, like us."

"Of course he is. It's the three of us, the four with Margaret. That's not such a bad life, is it?"

And all of Hal's want suddenly fell in on him, and he knew that he could only say everything if Guthrie would remember nothing. That he would never say, out loud, that love is hunger; that hope comes not on a full stomach but an empty one, one so empty it hurts. And so the only thing left was for the rain to wash everything away, stores and playgrounds and streets and homes, everything. But that would never happen either, Hal thought, and so the only thing left was for him to leave, alone, to get away as far and as quick as possible.

"Get some sleep, buddy."

He rolled over to push himself off the bed, but couldn't hold himself up. The room twisted and fell away, and Hal slumped back on the foldable bed, staring at the television, hating everything that moved, flat and pixelated, on its screen.

GUTHRIE SHOOK Hal awake just before midnight. He lay very still, watching Guthrie unwrap two pistols from newspaper.

"Only two? Hal doesn't get one?" Dixson asked.

"You don't get one."

"Why the hell not?"

"You said you wouldn't carry it. Why should I buy three?"

"But what if I had changed my mind?"

"What's changed? They change the law?"

"Heh, I guess not." Dixson looked at Hal, "If we get caught, all the boys with guns go away for armed robbery. Me, I'm just a bystander."

"But you'll be right there with us."

"Maybe I'm a hostage," he said, and winked.

Guthrie put a long barreled revolver in the back of his belt and covered it with his jacket. Hal tucked the snub nosed .38 into his pocket and followed them out to the car.

They stopped for beers to take the edge off, then drove past the end of Main, past the edge of downtown, out onto the two lane highways. The yellow lines scrolled up under the tires like a soft hand. Trees blurred past. Looking closely, Hal thought that he had passed through these woods a hundred times before. The landscape ground around him like unseen gears, the Mercedes spinning at the center. Guthrie made a three point turn in the middle of the highway and started back the way they had come. Dixson lit one off another. There was no sound, inside the car or out, other than the engine and the fuzzing rain.

They pulled into the Bi-Lo at a quarter past one. Guthrie circled the lot once, like they had made a wrong turn, then drove across the street and parked in the hotel lot. They waited until a police cruiser pulled into the Bi-Lo, right on time. The deputy drove slowly past the front doors, then parked under a street light, idling.

"Wasting gas," Dixson said. "That's tax money."

At one-thirty the sheriff disappeared up Main Street and the three men got out of the Mercedes. They crossed the street, skirting the lot and edging around the back of the building. Their shoes splashed the flooded alley. They waited while Dixson took a claw hammer out of his jacket and smashed a window in the delivery doors. Safety wires, embedded in the glass, caught and held, but Dixson twisted the hammer and tore them out.

"That looks like a weapon to me," Hal whispered as Dixson reached through the broken glass to unlock the bolt. "You'll get armed robbery sure as I will."

"I didn't think of that." He opened the door and, leaning back against the handle, threw the hammer onto the roof. "Rain washes away fingerprints," he said, winking again, but breathing heavily now.

They waited for their eyes to adjust. Inside, the store was inches deep in water. Security lamps cast the grocery aisles in a dim, lifeless light. Guthrie led the way, knowing exactly where to go, white wakes stirred up by his shoes. The store smelled like disinfectant and newsprint and the rising stink of the flood waters.

He stopped at a mirrored window at the front of the store and said to Dixson, over the hum of the freezers, "Give me that claw hammer."

"I left it outside."

Guthrie took the pistol from his belt. "Then give me one of those grocery bags."

"Paper or plastic?" Dixson asked. Nobody laughed.

"Shut up and give me that apron instead."

He wrapped his arm in the apron and, facing away, shattered the mirrored glass so it powdered and scattered at their feet. Without any signal from Guthrie, Dixson knocked the last bits clear, crawled through and came around to unlock the door.

Guthrie went straight through to the office, straight for the desk, straight to the drawer that Miss Bentley had described, and took out a cash box the size of a phone book. With a chisel from his pocket, he chipped the lock loose. The lid popped like a jack in the box and Guthrie pulled out a bank bag, a manila folder, and stack after stack of bills in neat rubber bands.

"Lord have mercy," said Dixson. "How much is it?"

"More than we can count, standing here."

Guthrie closed the cash box and tied the money in three plastic bags. Then he looked closely at his chisel edge, checking for nicks.

"I wouldn't worry about that too much, Guthrie," said Hal. "I expect now you can buy another one."

"That for Murph?" Dixson pointed at the manila envelope. "Looks like it."

"Aren't you just a little curious?" Dixson asked, taking a cigarette out of his pocket. He cocked the Zippo, but before he could light it, Guthrie said, "Hush. Not a sound."

Hal heard it too – a key in the door, at the far end of the room. The door swung open and a figure came in, a penlight shining in its hand. Dixson and Hal crouched behind two armchairs, but Guthrie stood with nowhere to go, rock-still beside the desk. His enormous green and brown poncho caught the penlight as it swung, distracted, around the walls, over the desk, into the empty open drawer. Then Guthrie cleared his throat. The man jumped and fumbled the flashlight, the little circle of light bouncing around the room before stopping on the round mouth of the pistol, then on Guthrie's face.

"Get that light out of my eyes," Guthrie said, turning on a desk lamp.

It was the manager. His shoulders were sloped beneath the open, unbuttoned collar of his raincoat, a thin white t-shirt underneath. Without the tie to point the way, he seemed rudderless. He turned off the penlight and folded down a black and white umbrella.

"Man, you've got some bad timing."

"It's the flood," the man said, looking up from the gun, trying to place Guthrie's face. He wiped his nose on his sleeve. "There are things I don't want to get washed away."

"I guess not."

"You mind putting that gun down, sir? I don't have one."

"How do I know that?"

"Why would I bring a gun to my own office?"

"Why would you bring a flashlight?"

The manager didn't answer, only reached slowly across the desk and lifted the lid on the cash box. He opened and closed it several times, as though it were a magic trick, a toy with a hidden drawer that would refill again. Then he sat down, his face blank.

"It's a lot of money to keep in a desk drawer," said Guthrie. "Might have been worth making a deposit, now and again."

"It's not for the deposit. I've been saving it."

"Why not save it in the bank?"

"It's not exactly mine."

"You stealing from your own store?" Hal asked from behind the chair. The manager started to look around, but Guthrie touched the man's chin with the gun.

"I'm only going to say this one time. There's no need for you to look at anyone but me."

"I've seen you already. I remember all three of you, from the store, from earlier."

"Now, why would you say something like that?"

"If you let me go, I swear I won't tell it was you."

"That's the best you can do?"

"Okay, I can do better. I can not remember. I know how to not remember." The manager leaned into the desk. "I don't remember all the time. I don't remember to deposit a check, I don't remember to pay a delivery boy."

"You must be a patient man."

"That's true, I am. It hasn't been easy," the manager said. "It's a small store, in a small city. I tried to build something here, but regional supervisors come and go, and they never remember me, either. They forget so easily, that after a couple years you start to wonder, what else will they forget? A quarter here, a dollar there."

"How long have you been saving? How much longer, before you could get out?" Hal asked.

"I don't want out. I want in, all the way," the manager said, not turning. "I was saving to buy the store myself. The franchise is looking to close locations anyway, so a couple of years ago I signed with financial backers. They said if I could come up with fifty grand, they'd back me for the rest."

"There's more than fifty grand here."

"Hell of a lot more," Dixson said.

"A man has to feed his family, doesn't he? And, as soon as I own the place, I won't want to skim."

Sweat shone on Guthrie's face. He wiped it, the shine vanishing under his hand. He chewed the inside of his cheek roughly, thinking, before he spoke.

"You should know something, mister. Murph Murphy wants you out."

"What did you say?" the manager asked, his voice hollow as the vacant store, as the cash box.

"Why else would he pay me to steal this?"

The circle of white from the penlight snapped up Guthrie's front to the manila envelope, then trembled on Guthrie's chest as the man started to cry, rubbing his cheeks with both hands, rubbing so hard Hal thought he might make them bleed.

"Oh my God. Am I going to jail?"

"I expect that's the plan."

"But it was their idea in the first place. They said it if I steal, it would make the store look unprofitable, and position us to buy it out."

"I expect they did."

"Oh God, I've got children," the manager said, getting louder. Guthrie set the barrel of the gun, almost gentle, against his cheek, and hushed him. For a few minutes there was only the man's crying, and the scratch of Dixson's lighter as he struck it, inhaled, exhaled. Then

Guthrie cleared his throat again.

"What do you want this old place for, anyway?" He sat on a corner of the desk, the gun barrel still touching the man's face. "By morning it'll have three inches of standing water."

"It's my store," the manager said. "No matter who holds the papers."

He bent forward until his forehead rested against the desk. Hal peeked from around the chair and watched as Guthrie, sitting over him, reached to wipe the man's tears away with his palm. Then his hand moved fast, hard, tearing the man's raincoat open down the front. Buttons bounced across the desk.

"What are you doing? God, don't shoot me in the chest."

"Sit still, dammit."

Guthrie ripped the t-shirt open, too, down to the belt, then tore open the manila folder with the barrel of the gun. Stapled papers spilled onto the desk.

"Don't do it," Dixson said. "You're pissing away five grand, not to mention pissing off the Murphys."

"Pick up those papers and don't say a word," Guthrie said. The manager looked at him. Guthrie stuffed the papers into the man's open shirt, against his pale skin. "Keep them dry enough so when you get home, you can burn them. Anybody finds those papers, they'll know you were here tonight."

"Oh God," the manager said. "Why?"

"What do you want to ask me that for?"

"You're right," the man said, backing out of the chair, buttoning the raincoat, getting the buttons all wrong, still backing toward the door. "I'm not looking," he said. "I can't see any of you." He covered his face with one hand and held the raincoat closed with the other. "I can't see anything."

They followed him to the door and watched him run, without his umbrella, through the rain. His car started and punched out onto Main Street, dropping red streaks from the brake lights onto the gleaming road.

"Damn fool forgot his umbrella," Guthrie said.

"I'll take it," said Dixson. "No use getting wet."

They hurried back through the store, Guthrie gripping the plastic bags in one hand and the pistol in the other. At the back door, Dixon raised the umbrella and splashed out, but Hal caught Guthrie by the hand. Holding it, he could feel Guthrie's pulse beneath his fingers.

"Sheriff's back in five minutes. Be quick."

"Oh Guthrie. What are you going to do?"

"Same as you. Go to the hotel and get some sleep."

"I mean about Murph. He might come after you."

"We'll tell him the papers weren't here. If that man is smart, he'll say he wants out of the bargain, on account of the flooding."

"If he's smart."

"Yeah, maybe I should have told him that," Guthrie said and stepped outside. His mouth was tight at the corners, and when he spoke it seemed to Hal that everything went quiet, that he had breathed the wind out of the sky. "Did you see all that money? There might be enough."

"Yes," Hal whispered.

"If not, maybe there are other ways to help Margaret."

"No."

"What no?"

Because Hal knew the way to help her was the straw and blender and baths, and turning her in bed, morning and evening, morning and evening, always the next day.

"We should go, Guthrie."

"That's what I'm saying."

"I mean away. From everything. All of it." Hal waved his hand like he was parting the rain, holding back the waters.

"Hell, Hal," Guthrie said, chuckling. "Where would you go?"

Guthrie turned and splashed toward the hotel. As Hal followed, his steps stuttering in backbeat to Guthrie's, he imagined creeks rising higher and higher, fed from deep unseen springs, from far-off rivers and oceans, rising as high as the sky, wiping the world away under the idiot face of the moon, leaving nothing.

THE NEXT MORNING, Hal was at the airport, sitting at the bar under the little rotunda. He had waited around baggage claim and the gift shop for more than an hour, without seeing anyone who looked right.

But now, he sat with his back to a man who was traveling alone. The man was about his age, unshaven, with a tired stare. Every few minutes he turned in his seat to catch Hal's eye.

Hal let him look, rubbing his chin as if he were lost in thought, slipping his fingertip into his mouth. He hated every moment of it, thinking that he might as well slip that finger on down his throat and puke all over the bar top. Hating it as much as he had hated wrapping the bundled cash in a plastic bag, then duct taping it to Margaret's arm. As much as he had hated pushing her into the glare of the emergency room lobby, locking the wheels of her chair and walking away fast to hide in the bushes outside, to watch until the orderlies found her. Telling himself that whoever finds her, finds the money. Will keep it for her, will care for her.

The man stood up from the bar and came over to him.

"Nice day," he said.

"It could be," Hal replied.

He forced himself to look at the man's mouth. And when the man stepped away toward the bathroom, looking back at him, Hal followed.

He stood at a urinal as the man went into a stall, waiting until they were alone. Then he knocked at the stall door. The man opened it, his pants around his ankles. Hal punched him hard in the face, once, twice, aiming for his eyes. The man fell backward against the cool tile and Hal grabbed at his shirt, pulling him upright to hit him again, aiming for the blood.

"If you follow me, I will find your wife, your friends, your boss, your preacher. I will tell them what you wanted," Hal whispered, his mouth inches from the man's ear. He fumbled through the man's pockets and found a wallet, pulled out his driver's license. "See this? I have it. I know your name, and I will use it." The man's eyes were shut tight, already swelling, and he shook his head so hard that blood spattered Hal's shirt. "If you follow me, if you take even one step in my direction, I will come after you for as long as I live, trailing ruin behind me."

He rummaged in the man's bag for the ticket. Checked the airline name, the flight and seat number, not bothering to search for the destination. He could hardly feel the paper between his fingers. He glanced again at the man's driver's license. The picture was close enough.

"I will not say I'm sorry to you," he told the man, bending low over him, shaking in his face. "I don't even know you. I will never say it."

He washed his hands as best he could in the sink and pulled the man's coat on, holding it closed over the blood. In the concourse he heard the intercom, found the gate, heard the final boarding call. He waited in line surrounded by people who were chatting, gathering children, texting loved ones that they would be home soon. He handed the ticket and the license to the attendant.

"I've had a haircut since that picture was taken."

Her smile was empty and quick, a move-along-please smile. He walked fast down the jetway. Words were printed on the carpet in scuffed paint. At the end of the tunnel was a staircase leading down to the tarmac. At the foot of the stairs was the blue and white airplane. And from there, wherever.

Behind him, a woman with heavy suitcases said, "Will you hurry up, please?"

But Hal stood without moving, would not even take the first stair, for no reason that he could think of.

the houses under the sea,
the dancers under the hill

i.

TATE'S NEW JOB ended simply. He was at his stool at the greeter's station, stamping museum passes for a group of students, when a shoplifter sprinted out of the gift shop. Tate strained up in his seat to shout for security. The boy looked back to shout, "Faster, old man," and didn't see the plate glass window. He must have thought it was a wide open, clean escape, still running even as his body crumpled mid-stride and fell to the lobby floor.

The neat rows of students broke and scattered as Tate shambled across the lobby, his hands trembling on his hips, and stood, laughing until the museum guard arrived.

Within an hour, a video was posted on YouTube: Tate, in his greeter's vest, stooping over the shoplifter and wagging a long finger in his face. The lens zoomed and Tate's fierce smile filled the screen, the big gums, the teeth small and sharp as milk teeth, white whiskers invisible against his flushed skin.

"Like a stupid bird," Tate said over and over, his laugh echoing in the stone lobby, the audio slightly out of sync.

When he came back from lunch for his afternoon shift, he found the museum director waiting. She showed him the video. Rewound, and watched it again.

"You're wearing a museum vest, Tate. That's not how we treat visitors." She pulled a scribbled pink slip out of her pocket. "Please leave your vest at the ticket counter."

Instead, Tate wadded the vest into a ball and pushed it into a garbage can outside of the employee entrance, then walked down the concrete steps toward the courthouse. He wanted to see Bailey, to tell her what had happened – how the kid got what he deserved, how there was a video on the Internet to prove it. But when he crossed High Street, he came upon a crowd of gawkers who had gathered to watch the ring of blue flashing lights circling the courthouse. People rummaged in pockets to snap photos with their cell phones. Tate pulled out his phone, too, and pushed redial.

"It's okay, Dad, we evacuated a few minutes ago," Bailey said when she answered. "A man snuck a gun past security and waved it around one of the courtrooms like an idiot, like a hero. Swearing that he'd kill someone, then himself, unless he was allowed a clear line of fire at the defendant."

"Don't tell me that. What father wants to hear that?"

"It's over now," she said. "But the Mayor is already in front of the news cameras, promising better security. So we're loading everything onto trucks and carting it down to the Choo-Choo hotel. Turning conference rooms into makeshift courtrooms."

He pictured Bailey somewhere in the crowd ahead of him, facing sirens and TV microphones with the other judges, her head poking out of the black polyester accordion folds of the robes. Directing moving crews as they loaded the witness stands onto flatbed trucks.

"I'm having a bad day, too, Bailey. I got fired." He said it as half-confession, half-plea, a family ritual.

"I heard," she said gently. "It doesn't matter. And anyway the timing is perfect, because the City will be looking for security temps. You can keep me company."

So as Tate climbed onto the city bus, he was glad he got fired; he had taken the museum job, after all, to be closer to the courthouse, now that Bailey was serving on the bench. As the bus swung under stoplights, he thought about the day, six month earlier, when Judge Bluford had chosen Bailey as his pro tem; the old judge was dying of cancer and said he'd be damned before he let a grey-haired pack of white wolves tell him whom he could, or could not, appoint to wear his robes. That it had done them good to call him, a black man, Sir, and it was high time they learned to do the same for a woman.

Bailey had been wearing his robes ever since. Bailey, who had never argued a criminal case, who had barely made partner in her firm, not even thirty years old.

"That's my Bailey," Tate had told the old Judge over the sound of the oxygen machine, "the only girl man enough for the job."

Bluford didn't reply, the tubes swinging slowly back and forth from his nostrils.

TATE'S ONE-ROOM apartment was at the far end of a cul-de-sac, in a house that had been built in the forties with fat footers and shake siding, a deep porch and wild rosemary bushes; when it was converted to studio apartments, the original, hand-waxed doors had been replaced with metal safety doors. The cabinets of the kitchenette were empty except for boxes of cereal and canned tuna with pop-top lids. The walls and shelves were a faint white, empty of framed photographs or paintings; the only color in each room was from layers of paint peeling around the door frames.

When his watch clicked nine o'clock, he appeared in the fleur-de-lys foyer of Bailey's office, a bagged peanut butter sandwich in each hand. He waited for her by the elevator, and when she came downstairs they walked the four blocks down Main Street – past the new loft housing; past tables set out in front of the bakery for sweet tea and microwave pastries, where secretaries talked all day about the God-it's-hot-if-you'll-excuse-my-language-summer-sun; past the Mr. Zip with its ferocious orange walls and green gasoline pumps, its bins of melting ice, its public pay phone with the receiver long since stolen. They turned into an alley and walked faster, hurrying out of the sun and into the shade of the Choo-Choo hotel.

At one end of the hotel's loading dock there was a break in the wall, where the brown brick facade ended in staircase of yellowed wood and a ragged plywood door. Bailey unlocked its chain, then closed it firmly behind them.

Inside the courtyard, they walked along the rows of Pullman train cars that had been parked in the hotel's gravel yard for four decades, wired and plumbed into permanent hotel suites. Tate could hear families behind the window blinds, watching pay-per-view movies or toweling off from the swimming pool.

"Your mother and I stayed here on our honeymoon," he said. "It cost a hundred dollars a night, and that was back in 1976."

"I guess you don't go on a honeymoon every day," she said, as if she'd never heard it before.

Suddenly a man shouted, from behind them: "Hey, you two. You're not supposed to be here."

They turned to see a bailiff in a dark uniform hurrying closer. Bailey waved.

"Oh, it's you, Judge," the man said. "I didn't know you out of your robes." He took off his hat and the sun hit his thick, pale, clean-shaven face. "I haven't had a chance to talk to you, since yesterday," he said. "But I'm glad to get a minute. I'm sorry as hell."

"Past is past," Bailey said.

"Not to me, Judge. I nearly resigned this morning."

"You can't do that, Ronald. Who would keep us safe?" As Tate watched, she reached out and touched the man's arm, above the sweaty crease of his elbow. "Ronald, I'd like to introduce my father."

The bailiff squeezed Tate's hand, too earnestly. "You should be real proud, sir."

"Of Bailey?" Tate said, and the bailiff grinned to hear her name spoken informally, like he was being let in on a secret.

"Dad's on our temporary security team."

"Welcome aboard, sir," the man said, leading them along the wall to a service entrance. From a closet inside the door, he brought out a blue baseball cap with the Choo-Choo logo screen printed across the crown, tucked a handheld radio into the cap and passed it to Tate.

"What about keys?" Tate asked.

"You won't need them," the bailiff said. "Just keep the walkie-talkie on, and let us know if you see anything out of the ordinary."

"What does ordinary look like?"

"Don't be smart, Dad. You'll figure it out," Bailey said, heading down the hall. Tate followed her, tracing the intricate carpet patterns with the toe of his shoe as he walked.

"You know why they make these designs so fancy?" he said, to Bailey's back. "The more fancy the patterns are, the better they hide dirt."

"Well, they're pretty, too."

She cracked the door to a conference room so Tate could peek in. He saw the jury box and witness stand set into place, families already starting to fill in rows of folding metal chairs.

"It took all night and all morning to set up," Bailey said. "We should have waited until tomorrow to reopen testimony, but City Hall insisted. Too many news anchors asking if justice is sitting on her hands."

She led Tate to the next door down the hall. It opened onto a hotel suite with the beds and desk and dresser removed, and Judge Bluford's battered oak desk set in their place. Bailey laid out the sandwiches.

"Why don't you ever sit in the Judge's chair?"

"Not mine to sit in."

"The Bench isn't yours, either."

"Come on, Dad, you know better than that," she said, sucking peanut butter off her teeth. "The Bench doesn't belong to anyone."

Tate watched her flip through notes from the day before, her mouth moving as she read. He stalked the room, flipping through the business cards stacked on the corner of the desk, the box of manila folders with her name scrawled in marker. There were moths folded like scraps of paper in the window sill. Bailey's chair squeaked on its hinges as she leaned forward, a tiny sound perfectly in tune with the muted coughs and voices from the room next door.

"This case is a nightmare," she said. "As far as I'm concerned, it can't finish fast enough."

"It'll end when you end it."

"If only it were that easy." She shook her head. "Anyway, I've got no business presiding over a jury. I was supposed to hear civil cases; I only said yes to this one because the docket was full. But right now I'd give anything for a sweet, simple divorce."

"Don't be cynical, Bailey," Tate muttered. "It's ugly."

"You think so?" she said, hand-cranking the window open, fanning herself. "When everyone went crazy, yesterday, when that man showed up with his gun and everyone lost their minds, there was a seven year-old girl in the witness box."

"The man with a gun was in your courtroom? You didn't mention that, before."

"She'll be back up there today," Bailey said, ignoring him. "Trying to put the right words together, but too young to understand what she's supposed to say. I know what she means. Everyone does. But it's not my job to understand, it's my job to get it on record. So I let the lawyers ask her horrible questions, two, three, four times." She ripped a page out of a perforated pad, the paper tearing with a dry rattle. "And every time she points at the defendant, she doesn't point at his face. She points lower, lower, while his smirk grows, like he doesn't care who sees." She sipped coffee from a mug. "And you say it's the cynic who's ugly?"

"It's not just your job to get it on record, Bailey. It's your job to fix it."

Tate knew all the testimony, the motions and counter-motions, because Bailey told him the details of every case at the end of each day. Sitting on the porch of his apartment building, he had heard the intimacies of dozens of divorces and custody cases. Blow by blow, fracture by fracture, families coming apart as lovers spun lies through the courtroom, as Bailey tried to unwind them, strand by strand.

So he had heard all about the allegations against a rich kid from the Bluffs. While she had talked, his mind had wandered to sunny Sundays when Bailey was young, how he used to take her joyriding up the mountain, down a two-lane road to the subdivisions overlooking the city. Among the new construction, houses dotting the woods, he would make a show of writing down telephone numbers off realtors' signs. Seeing his little sedan reflected in the wide expanses of windows, he would tell Bailey to wave, pretending that her reflection waved back from inside the house.

But last night had been different. Returning from the police station in the early afternoon, she had been silent, not wanting to talk about the case. Instead, she asked Tate to her townhouse for dinner, then, afterward, to sit up and read with her. She lay tucked onto a half-sofa with her stocking feet on the armrest; whenever he trailed off, she had shaken him awake, pulling from a stack of French detective novels, translations of Simenon opened to her favorite chapters. The stories were perfect, she said, for anyone fiddling with the law – reminders not only of *homo praesumitur*, but also that, at heart, anyone is capable of anything.

Standing at the window, she said, "She's only seven years old, for God's sake." Her voice caught. "Do you remember when I was seven? I get the years mixed up."

Tate shuffled through memories like photos jumbled out of a cardboard box. Bailey newborn in the incubator, safe beneath the hard plexiglass shell. Holding tight to her as he changed her diaper, bathed her, lifted her into the crib, squeezing her leg not to drop her.

But it was her seventh birthday that he remembered in perfect, unbending detail; it was the morning that her mother emptied half the bedroom into suitcases and left. The birthday cake was baked by an aunt instead, gifts were bought at the drugstore and hurriedly wrapped by neighbors. Standing against the wall while the others sang, Tate had scratched at an itch on his stomach. As Bailey blew out her candles, searching around for smiles, he had slipped out of the room to pull off his shirt in the bathroom mirror, tracing the spread of chicken pox that snaked around his middle and up his chest. By nightfall, his body was covered.

The doctor had prescribed Tylenol and quarantine, but as he shivered and cursed in his bed, his body smeared in egg yolk and linseed oil, he suddenly sat up. Crept down the hall, quiet not to wake Bailey, and into her bedroom. Knelt slowly, almost ceremoniously, beside her bed and buried his face in her pillow, resting his seeping pores against her soft cheek. Within a week she was covered in a rash that matched his own, feverish under the gaping scabs. But two weeks later, she was safe, forever. The innocent infected, and so inoculated.

For Tate, this changed everything. The first day Bailey had recovered enough to leave the house, he buckled her into the front seat of the car. Her mother had never allowed her to ride in the front seat, so she grinned at him, delighting, tuning the radio, until he turned the headlights off and sped the dark curves of a country road, she clutching the dashboard and whispering for him to stop, to slow down.

When she had a nightmare of dogs nipping at her heels, Tate searched the highway until he found a mound of fur and flesh at the side of the road. Taking her hand in the headlights and stretching it out to touch the putrid remains, then handing her a shovel from the truck, to bury it.

"You'll never be scared of dogs again," he said as she dug, the dirt at her feet flecked salt wet.

Now, as she stood at the window, he told her: "Sit down, Bailey, and finish your coffee."

"I have a different idea, a better idea," she said. "How about I take that box of case files and pour it out the window. Let anyone read them, anyone who might tell me what I should do."

"I already told you what to do," he said, but she looked past him.

"I should go," she said, reaching into the mirrored closet for the long, black judge's robes.

TATE SAT ONTO the yellow stairs, leaning backward against the plywood door. The sun poured, thick as rain, down the back of his neck.

Across the alley from where he sat was a fence topped with loops of barbed wire; behind the fence was row after row of port-a-potties, ready for rental – a constant target for kids in the neighborhood. They would come from blocks around, carrying matted blankets stolen from yard sales or dumpsters, draping them over the barbed wire so they could scramble up and over, already unwrapping the plastic from enormous fireworks. To laugh, the next morning as they walked to school, pointing at plastic doors blown off the hinges – the spattered explosions that fanned out, ten feet across the ground.

Tate's forehead was damp under the band of the Choo-Choo cap. The summer heat pushed down on the city like a sweaty palm, the street rising in hazy waves to meet it. Through the door behind him, he could see into the hotel's flower garden. Shadows of canvas awnings cut across parents drowsing in teak lounge chairs, and strobed children as they ran up and down the sidewalk. Goldfish fluttered from shade to shade in the pond.

On the far side of the garden, a woman struck one match after another, letting each flare and burn without lighting the cigarette that angled out of her mouth. She was younger than Tate, by ten years, but her face had a worn look, her body shapeless. As Tate watched, she stepped quickly along the sidewalk and, looking left and right, backed through the open door of a Pullman car.

Tate wrapped both hands around the radio, as if he was warming them by its battery. But instead of pressing the call button, he crossed to the suite and stepped in after her.

Inside, the train car was like any other hotel room. Sunlight striped the unmade bed through the Venetian blinds; clothes were rumpled on the floor. The woman bent over an open suitcase, a dozen twenty-dollar bills in her hand.

"Hey lady," Tate said, sharpening his voice. "Is this your room?"

The woman looked at Tate's blue cap, its chugging train logo bearing down on her. She folded the money, a reflex.

"I can explain."

Tate held up the walkie-talkie.

"Okay, so maybe I can't," she said, then added, without hesitation: "But if you haven't used that radio yet, maybe we can work something out." She spread two of the twenties on the bedside table.

"I think we should step outside."

"And I think it's better to talk right here. Too many cops, too many courtrooms outside."

"I should know. My daughter's the judge."

"Oh is she?" the woman asked. "Isn't that just my luck?"

Tate led the woman out of the room. For a moment he thought she might gather her skirt and run away from him down the sidewalk, but she only sat onto the wall of the flower bed. She arranged pleats around her lap and pulled a tattered pack of cigarettes from a hidden pocket; lit one, the tip clouding instantly over with ash.

"So your daughter is the lady judge?"

"She's not a real judge, she's just filling in for a sick man. But he chose her out of every lawyer in Chattanooga."

"She seems real enough, from where I sit," the woman said. "You should be proud."

"I keep hearing that."

Her cheeks hollowed around the cigarette's filter, like it was sucking back.

"You a judge, too?"

"I just told you, she's not a real judge."

"Oh right," she said. "Well, I couldn't do that job. It doesn't come natural to me. Hell, I even avoided jury duty, until now."

"You're a juror? Did you return a verdict?"

"Not yet. We're in deliberations."

Tate's hand went to the radio. "You shouldn't be out here," he said.

"It's okay. The bailiff said no smoking inside." For several minutes she sat without speaking, then shifted to face him. "Look at me, mister. Guess how I make my living."

Her nails were unpainted. The hands were smooth as pink plastic, except for the flaking browned knuckles where the cigarette butt nestled. Her hair was pulled back with a brown rubber band, every strand slicked so tightly that if the band broke, Tate thought, not one hair would shift out of place.

"Well?"

He didn't want to guess. "Waitress," he said, the first thing he could think of.

"In a restaurant? My wrists wouldn't hold up to carrying treys, although I've traded my knees for them." She twitched up the long hem of her skirt. Her knees were callused white, the skin rough, as if dusted with coarse powder. "I clean houses. Used to have five of them, up on the Bluffs."

"You rummage through their luggage, too?"

"Okay, fair enough," she said, laughing softly. "I'll tell you what. You put that radio away, for good, and I'll tell you a little something that might be able to help your daughter. I know things about that boy on trial, in there. Things I never told a soul."

"You're a juror. You can't discuss the case," Tate said, not wanting her to stop. Thinking of how he could sit on the porch with Bailey, that very night, dropping hints until he asked her to tell her everything.

"I used to clean his parents' house, years ago, back when he was a boy." She shook the pack and lit another. "He would sneak around after me, making messes where I'd just been. His mother would see him doing it, and send him outside. So he would hide in the bushes and throw rocks at my car. Not big ones, just big enough to scratch the wax. When I caught him, he said the car was so scratched already, it didn't matter."

She cupped her hands, not speaking for a moment, as if she held the things she was about to say inside of them.

"They had a party once, for his class from school. It was his idea, and his mother was so proud of him for being thoughtful. I stayed late to work it, pass out cupcakes and clean up, and after all the games and popcorn what do you think I heard? One of the girls saying that she'd show them a thing or two, out back of the shed. She did it, too. I watched from the upstairs window as she dropped her shorts and the boys pointed, snickered. Then, out of nowhere comes that son of a bitch, that kid, swinging a yellow Wiffle ball bat, and smacks her across the backside. He hit her good, too. I could see the color coming up on her thigh."

She paused for effect, framed by the flower bed.

"I rushed downstairs to take the bat away, to drag him into the house, but he was already there. Standing with his back against the kitchen wall, with that girl. She had one hand pressed against the welt on her leg, her eyes dripping anger and hurt and shame. But she was there to collect. And as she watched, he dropped the bills on the floor, one by one. Laughing as she bent to pick them up, saying that it's fun to watch girls cry. Asking me if I was going to cry, too."

She inhaled the smoke like it was cool water, her head back, and crushed the cigarette against her shoe.

"That's why I didn't skip out on jury duty, this time. As soon as I heard he got arrested, I started praying I'd get a summons. And the second I sat down in the juror's box, I started praying that he would recognize me, and remember. Wipe that grin right off his face."

She stood stiffly, with effort, specks of ash falling from her fingers, invisible on the sidewalk.

"You've seen them houses, up there, shining gold as the sunrise. Everybody wants a house like that. But they can't live there without thinking they deserve to. Without thinking they deserve whatever they want. Once upon a time, mister, I was afraid of them, that they'd catch me doing something I shouldn't and I'd be out on my backside. But then I understood: they don't see me, they don't even notice I'm there. So, maybe I should make them take notice."

As the sky broke into evening, a long stream of first shift workers passed the open plywood door, walking up the alley away from where they sat in the garden. Crossing the traffic on Main Street, they climbed over knee walls or sat down at bus stops. One man stopped to rinse his face in a birdbath before disappearing around the corner.

"Holy Lord God," she said, her eyes upward. "That little girl face and those soggy eyes and any fool can see that she's not fit to answer such questions. You tell your daughter that judge to make it stop. Tell her I know he hurt that little girl, too. I just know it. That it's okay for her to hurt him back."

Tate stood up.

"She'll fix it," he said. "I told her to."

"Well you better tell her again," the woman said.

Through the open door, he could see the dim outlines of the near

Appalachians. Overhead, a small, irregular object – plane or bird or planet – wound its shadow up the street.

"After she turned seven, I was her father and mother both," Tate said quietly. "I remember standing for hours, listening to her breathing through the bedroom door, wondering how I was going to teach her everything I know, and everything I don't know, too. I would hear her sleeping, peaceful, and think that children must see something clearly, must have some knowledge that escapes us once we're grown. A secret that they know, only they don't know how to say it."

He looked at the woman, but she was fishing in the cigarette pack with her fingers.

"Then she got the chicken pox. One night, when her fever was its worst, she couldn't lay still. I went into the bedroom and she had kicked the sheets off the bed, and her legs were shaking like she was pretending to dance. I told her to stop, but she couldn't, looking up at me, her face sorry. We didn't have a car then, so I carried her to the bus stop, to the hospital, her head hot against my chest. That was when I knew that there isn't anything good, and pure, and noble that children know. Children are nothing but a fear-shaped hole, waiting for life to fill them up."

As Tate talked, his face tightened, the old man skin shrinking around his teeth.

"I spent eleven years teaching her all I could. And the day she turned eighteen, I sent her to college. Made sure she got on the Greyhound safe, and then I cut her off. I wouldn't reply to her letters, I wouldn't answer when she called. Once, I picked up the phone by mistake and had to pretend it was a wrong number, saying, Hello? Who's there? before I hung up."

The woman whistled between her teeth.

"But she panicked. Ran away from college, bought a bus ticket home and showed up in the front yard. Grabbed the front of my shirt, asking Why? What's the matter with you? But I would only tell her what she should have already learned. That the strong daughter, the beloved daughter, learns two things – first, that she can trust her daddy to take care of everything. Second, that she can't."

"Hold on a minute, that isn't love."

Tate looked at the woman. She was bent over, twisting cigarette butts into a crack in the sidewalk.

"The hell it isn't," he said.

"If it smells like love, it's love. If it doesn't, mister, then it's something else. Maybe something better. You wanted to make her strong. You said so."

"And it worked. Look at her. Judge Bluford said she's the only girl in town, man enough to sit the Bench."

"Sure it worked. All I'm saying is, sometimes you've got to choose between being kind and being right. And if you want to make them strong, there's no better teacher than hate."

"Make her hate me, my own daughter? Don't you see that can't be true?" he said, feeling the bones of his face give way, his mouth slack around the words, thinking: yes, that's it exactly.

The woman dropped the empty pack onto the sidewalk.

"Look here, mister. I'm out of smokes. I should get inside, before I get in trouble." She stifled a yawn. "About the money, I know what you're thinking. Stealing is a sin. But there's sin, and there's stupid. And if a person is stupid enough to leave their hotel door unlocked, they turn it into a welcome mat."

"Just go," Tate said, in a voice without breath behind it.

"Okay, but if you don't want those other twenties, I could put them to use."

She slipped back into the Pullman, leaving Tate looking around the garden, his eyes searching for the sounds coming from the distant swimming pool, buzzing insects in the garden, trucks out in the street. Anything to look at, to stare at, not to close his eyes and see Bailey's face at eighteen, her eyes dark with tears, in the front yard. Not to think about twisting her away from him as she sobbed, as she vomited into the bushes.

The woman came out of the train car with her hands in her pockets, just as the bailiff appeared around the corner.

"Where in hell have you been?" His wide, pasty mouth was almost shouting. "I've been looking everywhere for you."

"You said no smoking inside."

"I meant don't smoke at all. I didn't mean for you to sneak off."

"Nobody's sneaking," she muttered and followed him around the corner. Tate followed them, a few steps back, to Bailey's makeshift Chambers. Tate waited outside until the bailiff came out, alone.

"All I said was, there's no smoking in the building," he told Tate. "I thought she would go into the washroom, like everybody else. You remember that, sir. You remember it to your daughter."

Half an hour later, Bailey declared a mistrial and came into the hallway, the robe already draped over her arm.

"Dammit, Dad. What were you thinking?"

"This is my fault?"

"You're my father. I got you this job. When you shit, it splashes my shoes."

"You can't talk to me like that, Bailey," he said, snapping his fingers and pointing at her. "No matter how old you get, you'll always be my child."

"Your daughter," she said. "There's a difference." She passed the judge's robe to the bailiff, who held the door open without looking up. "Let's go, Dad. No sense in staying here."

They walked the hallways and the gravel yard. When they reached the plywood door, it was still propped open.

"Don't blame me. Nobody gave me a key," Tate said, but Bailey pretended she hadn't heard.

The alley was deserted again. Tate thought jealously of the first shift workers, already in bed or slumped in front of televisions, not facing a long walk home. He muttered under his breath, repeating words over and over to himself, folding the air with an open hand.

"Speak up, Dad."

"I say, you call that justice? You had a job to do."

"I did my job. That woman was out of sequester for fifteen minutes. She was talking with the judge's father. It's unfair, by law."

"So he goes free. Is that fair?"

"Of course not. But yes, he goes free. For now, anyway." Her voice was paper-thin. "It's not what I wanted, Dad. If it were up to me, I don't know what I would do to him. Maybe something awful."

"It was up to you, Bailey. You should have stayed strong."

She squinted down the street, past him. The sun was setting at her back, shining red on his face.

"That's me," she said. "Your strong girl. The beloved girl."

"Don't you put that on me," he said, swallowing the words, one by one, as he spoke them.

She stepped toward him.

"Dad, do you remember when I was a kid, and you would fall asleep in the hallway outside my room? I would crawl out, and I would try to fall asleep on the floor beside you. But I never could. I was too excited, my face against your sleeve, the tips of my fingers on your arm, watching your snores slow down to nearly nothing. You seemed so strong to me, then. And I remember thinking that if I could study you, close enough, then I might be able to be strong, too."

She touched his arm, feeling that her hand was very small against it. But he pulled backward in a complicated shuffle, backing against the chain link fence. At that moment, on the street behind them, a car honked its horn softly.

The car was the color of wet brass, wide and close to the ground, with twin grills that flared like nostrils. It braked, engine idling, and the driver's door opened. A man stepped out, tall, with his sleeves were rolled high above broad hands. His tie was loosened around his collar: a hammock, a low smile.

"That you, judge?"

He held out his hand. Bailey hesitated, then took it.

"We thought so. We wanted to stop and tell you, personally, how pleased we are."

Bailey held on to the man's hand, pumping it up and down, as if she couldn't let go.

"Son, come out and thank the lady judge."

The boy unfolded out of the back seat – first the buffed black shoes, legs splayed wide, then the long torso and face, the carefully tousled hair. He's just a kid, Tate thought. But he was taller than Bailey, and as he looked down at her, his eyebrows met his nose in a deep shadow, the eyes beneath like watching mouths, red rimmed, hungry.

"God bless you, Judge," he said, his lips wet on the words.

"It wasn't my decision. I was following the law."

"Whatever you say," the father told her. "But by our count, that's twice in two days."

Tate pushed against Bailey, trying to take the man's hand. But she leaned backward, pressing him against the fence. He thought about the backdrop of port-a-potties, behind him, as the man and boy watched him, standing against their shimmering car.

"Now, Bailey," Tate said roughly. "How about you let your old man out from behind your skirts?"

The man laughed. "The way we see it, that's not a bad place to be." He clapped his son's back, hard; the boy looked at his father, abrupt and angry.

A woman's voice came from inside the car, begging. "Can we go? I can't stay here another moment."

"If Momma's not happy," the man said, and put his hand onto his son's head, jostling him back into the back seat. The car pulled ahead and away, the boy's hand waving from the back window.

Bailey let her hand drop. Overhead, the streetlights crackled on.

"What did he mean, twice in two days?"

She shook her head. "You wouldn't understand."

"Don't be ridiculous. I'm your father."

He wriggled out from behind her, and they walked on through the blue wash of dusk. Tate bunched his collar up, thinking that he should get home before the air turned chill. But as they turned the corner, they saw the big, brassy car parked beneath the high rain roof of the Mr. Zip. The three of them – father, boy, mother – were inside at the counter. Bailey hung back, but Tate went in. He crossed the store to the refrigerator shelves set into the far wall, pulled open a glass door and watched through it. The man was arguing loudly with the clerk, demanding to know why the store doesn't stock champagne. Tate picked up a six-pack of beer and walked toward the front, rounding the shelves to look at the boy's mother. She stood, staring down at a bottle of ginger ale and a carton of eggs in her arms. The fluorescent light slashed deep lines in her cheeks, and shaded her hair with streaks of pencil. Wrinkles filled at the corner with dribbles of saliva that she did not bother to wipe away.

"Hey, I know you," the clerk called out. "You're that woman on the news." Tate looked up to see that he was pointing at Bailey, who cringed in the doorway. "You're the lady judge."

"Sure, that's her," the boy's father said. "She's the reason we're hunting champagne. To toast her."

"If she's the knight in shining armor, then you're the damsel in distress," the clerk said, pointing at the tall boy, the son. "Both of you, together, here in the Mr. Zip. Can I take your picture? I want to post it on my Facebook."

Tate pushed forward to the counter, the six pack cold in his hand. "Why are you calling her a knight in shining armor? She didn't even do her job right."

"This is her father," the tall man whispered to the clerk. "I guess he isn't impressed."

"For God's sake, impressed with what?"

"Didn't she tell you? And even if she didn't, how could you miss it? I thought old men always watch the news."

Tate looked at Bailey, thinking of how she had invited him to her townhouse the night before – read with me, she had said, stay up with me – until long after the six o'clock, ten o'clock, eleven o'clock broadcasts were over.

"Wait a minute, I've got a copy of the newspaper," the clerk said. Bailey came up the aisles to take Tate's arm, to tug him gently toward the door, but he pushed her away. "It doesn't matter, I know it by heart. The whole city knows it. Man showed up in her courtroom with a gun, but nobody noticed. The guards were distracted and the lawyers were busy with their yellow pads, just like on TV. And before anybody realized, this asshole was standing at the Bench, with a pistol in her face."

"Please Daddy, don't listen," Bailey whispered in Tate's ear.

"Everyone gasped: Oh no, not the Judge. Only she isn't the Judge, is she? The paper said the usual Judge is down at the hospital, sucking chemo from a plastic tube. She just happened to be sitting in his seat. Wrong place, wrong time.

Bailey stopped pulling at Tate, hid her face in her hands.

"They say he pushed the gun so hard against her forehead that it left a mark, and shouted that if everyone did what he said, he'd let her go. That he only had one bullet in the gun, and that it could either be for the judge or it could be for the crazy shit sitting in the defendant's chair. That if they would all just step aside, then the one bullet would be enough for him and his little girl to put this behind them, forever. And you know what? Everybody did. Witnesses, lawyers, everybody took a step away from the defendant. From you," he said, grinning and pointing. "Nobody was going to lift a finger."

"I can't take any more," said the wife, the mother.

"You shut up," her husband told her.

"But not the Judge," the clerk said. "She slowly rose, and came down from the Bench. Walked across the courtroom. That man with the gun was watching her the whole time, following her, as she pushed, unhurried, past tables and chairs and people, until she came to the defendant. Then she lifted her robes and wrapped them around him, pulling him in close, covering him. The man was right behind her, the gun resting behind her temple now, and everyone waited for the shot, for the burnt chalk smell in the air. But it never came. Nothing happened, except the pistol clattering to the floor, the guards rushing the man, the courtroom spilling into the street."

"I'm going to be sick," the mother said.

"Oh why don't you grow a pair?" said her husband. "Go wait in the car."

Bailey came close but Tate pulled away from her.

"You're damn right I don't understand," he said.

"I wanted to tell you, but I didn't know how."

"That's not what I taught you. You should know better, helping someone like that," Tate said.

"You better watch yourself, old man," he shouted back.

"I didn't do it for him, Daddy, or even for the man with his gun. It was for her. I didn't want her to go through something she couldn't forget."

And Tate saw everything: the girl in the witness box, staring up as her father held the sharp end of a gun between a Judge's eyes, knowing that he was ready to rip their world to pieces. Her eyes following Bailey across the room, as she lifted the robes to wrap the man who hurt her. As she made it all stop, at least for a moment.

"You should have gone to the girl, Bailey. You should have covered her little eyes, while her father did what he had to do."

"That's what you would have done. Not me."

He chopped the air between them, with his hands. "No, you too. You know better, Bailey. How could you save him?"

"I could because I had to, Dad. I had to because I could."

Bailey leaned into him, but Tate shook his head wildly, his thin arms quaking the glass bottles. He swung at her with his free hand, catching her cheek. She fell backward as he threw the cardboard pack of beers wide, wrapping his fingers around the neck of a single bottle, letting the others drop to the floor. He pushed her backward until her feet slid, until she slipped, until she fell into the shattered glass. The last thing she saw was her father, the bottle raised over his head, rushing the boy. Then her head hit the floor with a loud sound.

ii.

BAILEY LAY flat and blinking. As the spinning room rocked to a stop, she listened for voices, but there weren't any. Only a brittle quiet, thin but absolute, unbreakable. Then the smells of blood and beer saturated the air and she sat up, dripping. Her leg was cut; it was not deep, but red swirled out of her, curling through the puddled beer.

The store was empty. Bailey stood and looked carefully from aisle to aisle, crouching to peer under shelves. She called her father's name, then cursed him softly. The front doors parted automatically in front of her. She walked outside and saw that the big car was gone. In its empty space was the ginger ale bottle, its cap cracked and hissing. Eggs were smashed like runny suns against the curb.

Bailey heard a sound from around the corner and ran to it, calling, "Dad," calling, "Tate," but it was not her father. It was the boy's mother, kneeling in a patch of grass. She fell sideways and Bailey rushed to catch her, holding her upright against the side of the building. The woman's wrinkled face was shining, streaked with tears and vomit.

Bailey hushed her in a single, long, seemingly endless breath, her fingers stroking the woman's grey hair back from her face. The woman retched again, and Bailey dropped clumsily to her knees, to cradle the woman's head close to her chest, softly rocking with the arrhythm of the heaving shoulders, until the smell overpowered her, and she gagged, and they heaved violently together.

DOWN the stairs, and
down the stairs first thing newspaper mornings,
last thing garbage nights.
Back up for dinner or forgotten keys or bed,
down again to check the mail for checks,
to phone my sister Cookie in Memphis from the pay phone,
ask: How's the flu and, Did you get my letter?
Down past, out and in.
Up stairs for remembering, downstairs for making.
Down the stairs and into
Bess. She says, from her doorway:

> "Did you ever sit thinking with a thousand things
>   on your mind? Thinking about someone."

She only wants to grab and pull me back between the sheets.
Too many nights down, nearly passing her door,
but stopping to knock.
Then, long before light, the long way back up.

Down into regret and joy. Even regret a joy
to busy lonely nights,
my mind slow with TV movies and microwave dinners
and promises I practice in the quiet after.

She could be only a habit. Like any habit I could break.
Neighbors should lock doors, close curtains. But she says:

> "Don't you hear me baby, knocking on your door?
> Don't you?"

As she squeezes a single tear from her eye, watching it
drop spinning mascara black like some forgotten sun
to splash the concrete floor, sings:

> "It's the only way, baby, I can get these thinking blues
> off my mind."

Up the stair stair stair stair stair stair stair stair stair stair.
The handrail is thin enough for my fingers to wrap around.
I lose skin off my knuckles on the cinder blocks, every time.
Once I heard that our bodies make all new skin
every twenty-four hours.
We are born with each sun and die with the moon,
leaving trails of us on walls, between sheets,
breathed and blown by each other, on every stair.

The geographic center of America, once I heard,
is somewhere in the flats of Kansas.
A spring bubbles there, but its water is soured from
cross-country campers dumping their shit tanks.
I had a friend once who had a camper,
drove it clear across the country.

I don't want to remember this.

"Do you hear me, baby? Have you got the nerve to say you
don't want me no more?"

Her words fill the narrow, empty, breezeless stairwell.
I wish I could paint the stairs the color of the street and sky.
I wish I could hang a bulb by a worn cord,
swinging naked,
to set the mood.
I wish I could step outside, past her door,
talk to kind neighbors, stoop afternoons,
wave to families driving past.
I wish the pipes would rust through, crack and burst,
that Bess would run, squealing over her laughter,
upstairs to my apartment.

We would go together down
and up, down and
up again, carrying dripping heavy cardboard boxes
of photos, bills long past due,
an old rug beat thin as paper,
dragging the wet-dry vac to erase all trace of our footprints.
Tell someday children that it all
changed when her apartment flooded two inches deep, two.

Change for the bus bulks my pocket.
I saved for months, it might get me far as Memphis.
I could overnight with Cookie, borrow more change
for the Greyhound's thirsty tank, for tires that spin
bridges that span the Mississippi.
The river at St. Louis nearly a mile wide and muddy,
what starts a trickle somewhere up North, I never.

Then Kansas flat as a bed sheet, a four-square state,
the dry heat heart of the nation. Watch that bubbling spring,
blue and big as any ocean,
blue as thinking,
big as Bess standing in the doorway,
as beautiful as
the world is wide as
the world is deep as
the world is angry as
the world is sharp as
the world is soft as
the world is stale as
the world is sweet,
calling:

    "Take me back, baby, try me one more time.
     Don't you hear me, baby?"

Bess, I do.
For better or worse, for
her grinning and dragging the wet-dry vac
up stairs on its retractable cord,
sucking balled cobwebs into the plastic tube.

THE FIRST TIME SHE FELL, Anna thought: maybe everything that is beautiful starts ugly. The three stories of brick rushing past, once nothing but sand. The snow, rising spotless to meet her, once gasoline-swirled puddles in parking lots. Even her own body, twisting through the air toward the ground, once a raisin-faced newborn, with all her future joy and fear and sex and death out on the birthing table for anyone to see. Not yet repressed deep into the DNA.

The paint can hit the ground before she did, popping open in a splash. She lay on her side in the paint and snow for a long time before anybody noticed.

When the EMTs bent over her, they made notes on the scene: cables dangling from a maintenance panel on the steeple, a wet brush. As they stuck her with the first needle, Anna muttered through the morphine: "Damned bricklayers, always throwing up buildings, stealing pieces of sky. Cutting the uncluttered blue into geometries of cornices and ridgepoles. When this was a vacant lot, empty except for grass and trash, people walking the neighborhood would stop to stare at the morning moon reflected in broken pieces of glass; night in day, sky in ground, all crammed into half an acre of nothing much. Now, there's nothing here but a building."

The EMTs were used to ramblings from the gurney, and went about their paperwork.

A week later, after the IVs and skin grafts and nausea, Anna came back to the church. Two days of blowy, late March rain had melted the snow, leaving only bumpers of blotchy brown and white at the curb. But a long streak of mismatched paint showed on the brick, covering over the places where she had bounced off the wall on her way to the ground. The doctor said that this very well could be what had saved her – the weight of her body pressing into the rough brick as she fell, the friction of her fighting gravity.

"SIMEON SCHAEFFER?"

"PFC."

"I'm aware of your rank," said the petty officer seated behind the desk. "Sit down. I'll let him know you're here."

Simeon sat on the bench, his back touching the wall at the shoulder blades. Like the wall has just been painted, he thought, and my uniform is stuck to it at these two points.

Ten minutes later the officer called him. "You, Schaeffer. Go into the first room and strip down to your shorts. He'll be in soon."

"Do you have any idea how long it'll take?" Simeon asked. "My sergeant said to report in an hour."

"You won't wait long."

"I could come back tomorrow."

"Go into the first room, private," the man said. "He's with other patients, he'll be there in a minute."

The heels of Simeon's shoes struck the floor slowly, trying to mark intervals of one second exactly. He closed the door to the small room and stripped, feeling his shoulders come square out of the undershirt. He thought about how much he would miss wearing the uniform. Before leaving for basic training, he had worn MultiCam to his high school reunion, among the bow ties and suspenders of his old classmates, stopping to chat with spotty, spangle-eyed middle schoolers in the halls. Glad to see old friends, to meet the wives and children on their arms. Glad that they politely steered clear of questions about Betsy, asked about life in the Army, avoided all talk of wars.

"At ease," the medical officer said when he arrived, not glancing up from the chart in his hand.

"Schaeffer, PFC?"

"Yes, sir."

He flipped the chart. "How long have you been in?"

"Six months." Simeon stood awkwardly at ease in his underwear, his legs jutting out of the white briefs.

"Hometown?"

"Atlanta."

The officer smiled at the chart, a brief flash. "You're old, private. Not like most recruits, just out of high school. Where'd you come from?"

"Seminary, sir."

The officer tapped his teeth with the tip of the pen. Ink rubbed off on his lip.

"Lie back."

He palpated Simeon's abdomen with circling fingers.

"I knew a sculptor, once, who went to seminary just so he could say he dropped out. The failed priest factor is good with the ladies. Very Van Gogh."

"I graduated," Simeon said as the man dug a thumb into his kidneys, his liver.

"So why not enlist as a chaplain?"

Simeon held his breath with each deft poke, answering in short spurts. "I don't know, sir. Lots of reasons."

The officer's hand stopped, but didn't lift away from Simeon's stomach.

"This isn't small talk, Schaeffer. I asked you a question."

"Yes, sir. A chaplain has a ministry of presence, going where the soldiers go. No offence, but that didn't seem like enough. I wanted to do what the grunts do. To be with them, I have to be one of them."

The officer unwound the stethoscope from his neck. Simeon breathed deeply when the man told him to, thinking: how can he listen to my heartbeat and my lungs and my answers all at once?

"I get that, I respect that. But why the Army at all? There's always a story, and usually a girl. Were there girls, at this seminary of yours?"

Simeon thought of the letter folded at the bottom of his dresser drawer, back in barracks. Of Betsy's handwriting, large and looping and desperate; words he read every night, following the pen line with his eyes to try to burn them into the paper, to keep them from disappearing. He thought of standing on the balcony of their room, watching her walk up the icy hill above the ski lodge. She was wearing nothing but ski boots, carrying a baking sheet she had stolen from the hotel kitchen; a man whose name he didn't know, wearing nothing but boxer shorts, was following her. His wife of three months, walking naked on a hill with a man he'd never meet.

And then they came sledding down fast, Betsy out front, snow pluming high behind the sides of the tray, her eyes shut. She twisted to a stop under the balcony and stood up, bleeding from her knuckles. The man, close behind on his tray, smashed into the wall of the lodge, jumped up and hurried inside, bleeding down his thigh. But Betsy stood, weaving like a tall stack of plates, her skin spotted with the cold, not bothering to cover herself, staring up at Simeon on the balcony. From another window, a camera flash blinked the snow around her into painful white. That was the last time he ever saw her. As he lay under the doctor's hands, he wondered: how can that happen, in this day and age, that you can never see someone again?

"I just needed a change, sir."

"Well, you got one."

"At least, here, I know what to do."

"Explain. Cough."

Simeon coughed so deep in his throat that his lungs rattled.

"Here, there's always someone to tell me exactly what to do. And when, and where, and for how long."

The officer frowned. "We don't want robots, private. We want you to think."

"Just not for ourselves."

The officer chuckled. "You may have a point."

Simeon didn't want to talk any more. "It really was that simple, sir. I needed a change."

"Well, let's see if you're about to get another one."

As the doctor peered through a plastic lens into Simeon's eyes, the burnished metal disc of the stethoscope dangled in front of his mouth, as if recording every word. Simeon could still feel the cold prints where the disc had rested against his skin.

"Passed out three times in six months?"

Simeon nodded. The third time was less than a week before, rushing the sand pits, battling life-size dummies hung from ropes. Simeon had slashed with the same field knives carried by thousands of recruits before him, gashing throats and bellies, the mannequin enemy bleeding sawdust onto his face and hands, into his mouth. He collapsed. When he woke he was face-down, hands sunk deep in the hot sand, digging for the cold soil that he new must be somewhere underneath. When he woke again, he was in the base hospital, a dozen interns and nurses crowding the bed. He lay very still, thinking that he had never felt more a part of the Army than at that moment, with them grouped around him, lifting his eyelids and poking in his ears, plumping his veins, reviving him.

"You tested clean for drugs; your CT scan is clear. Your sergeant said you just overheated. Are you hydrating?"

"Yes sir, confirmed by my sergeant. He says if a soldier dies from heat stroke, it will be a black mark on his record."

"Not only his." The officer scratched his temple with the pen, leaving staccato dashes just outside his hairline. "So do you like the idea of fighting, Schaeffer?"

"I'm sorry, sir?"

"Does it inspire you, thrill you? Are you the hammer of God, bringing judgment on the infidel?"

"No, sir. I don't want to do that. Not unless I have to."

"You mean, unless you're ordered."

"Right. Unless I'm ordered."

"But it must at least inspire you. Remember, I said inspire." He waved the stethoscope in the air like a baton, like a bayonet. "You know, 1812 Overture, your personal handheld cannon blasting in cadence."

"That's not why I joined," Simeon said.

The doctor lowered the scope in denouement, laughing aloud. The earplugs slipped out of his ears and snapped together around his neck.

"Okay, private. I get a lot of bullshitters in here, kids eager to get back into civilian clothes. It's my job to report on whether they are a danger to society. Are you a danger to society?"

"No, sir."

"Then we're finished."

Simeon reached for his clothes, getting up.

"How much longer do I have?" he asked.

The doctor grinned.

"Don't sound so worried, Schaeffer, Jesus isn't calling. Get your heart checked once a year, take the meds they give you. You can have a long life; you just can't have it in the Army."

"Sorry, sir. I mean until I'm discharged."

"Oh, that. Four or five days, at the most. Want me to recommend a desk job?"

"Thank you, sir, but I'm going to reenlist as chaplain."

"No, you aren't. A chaplain's job is to carry soldiers in combat, not for them to carry you."

As the officer walked into the hall, Simeon leaned after him.

"Sir, excuse me, sir?"

The man was surprised at being called back, the next soldier's chart already open on the clipboard.

"What will I do?" Simeon asked.

He paused, thinking.

"Can't you go home?"

Simeon thought of flying into Atlanta, walking the airport terminal without the uniform. Feeling as naked in civvies as if he were wearing nothing but the white briefs, everyone staring or awkwardly looking the other way. He shook his head.

"Give it some time, son. Pick a city that's close but not too close, familiar but not too familiar. Smaller than home, more manageable." He laughed again, looking at Simeon's expression. "And don't worry,

I'm sure you can find someone who will tell you exactly what to do."

Simeon began to dress even before the door closed. He unshaped the undershirt from the hanger, feeling the cotton catch against his short, coarse hair as he pulled it over his head. Next, the collared, starched white shirt, its six buttons sliding into place.

His fingers worked fast, hoping that an hour hadn't passed, so he could report to the sergeant on time. But as he walked from the clinic to his barracks, he found himself refusing rides from passing trucks, slowing his walk, hoping that he was late. That the sergeant would shout at him, roaring inches from his face.

And if he tells me to scrub the floors, I will do it.

And if he gives an order for a thousand pushups, I will do it.

And if he tells me to stand stock-still in the center of the room, I will do it.

THE NEW CHURCH BUILDING was three stories of red brick on the Southside of downtown, built on the site of a once-grand hotel that had been passed over by the renovation revival that swept Chattanooga for much of the 1990s. The property owners, taking the long view, had opted instead for swelling plywood in the windows and, eventually, a controlled blast at the base of its load-bearing columns.

The lot sat empty, rubbled, collecting trash for a decade. Until, one Sunday morning, Braxton Jackson muscled a picnic table onto it, stood on the sagging wood boards to preach an impromptu sermon. Forty-four, with a thick brown goatee and eyes small and wary as snails, Braxton had once been a high school soccer star, but his body had slipped into stubborn atrophy. When he leaned forward against the picnic table to pray or lay out the communion meal of Bunny Bread and grape juice, his stomach lipped over his belt. His voice however, was Southern syrup, his handshake reassuring, his smile wide under an immaculate baseball cap. He held hands with anyone who would hold his; heads bowed, eyes closed.

Sunday after Sunday, he stood on the picnic table in the empty lot, barking out sermons about genocide and global warming, Y2K and the Towers, rumors of AIDS replaced with rumors of West Nile and mad cow and SARS and bird flu, pesticide on our plates and bubbles in bank accounts. Our parents thought they lived in a simple time, he said, afraid only of war and fear itself; but it's we who are simple. The only thing we have to fear is everything. The Middle East, the Far East, Wall Street, nuclear fallout, chemical spills, bacteria, antibacterials, public schools, private schools, other churches. We're all baby beasts, he said, cowering in the corner, facing annihilation at every moment. Put locks on your doors, on your children, on your water and air.

Membership skyrocketed. When it hit fifty people, Braxton bought a speaker's podium and rented space at a local coffee shop, for $50 a week plus cleanup. When it hit one hundred, he bought silver plates for the offertory and splurged on gluten-free bread and ten-dollar wine for communion. Interns started to arrive from seminaries around the country, come to build strong curricula vitae as junior pastors cum entrepreneurs cum community organizers. Young men and women in jeans and flip-flops sat beside blue-haired women from the neighborhood.

Then one of the old women died, willing the vacant, rubble-strewn lot to the congregation, along with two houses that were to be sold immediately, with the proceeds going toward construction. The houses brought a surprising amount, enough for Braxton to form a capital campaign committee, secure loans, and buy a brass shovel.

Anna walked by the construction site every morning. Watched the floor shape out of slab, rebar skeleton upward, bricks rise against the blue. Ten floor-to-ceiling windows of stained glass were set into the walls, technicolor prophets veined with lead. The newly-laid sod smelled like ashes.

The day a prefab steeple was assembled on the lawn, she stood at the fluttering caution tape, asking Braxton why a church needed a building, why a building needed a steeple. Braxton told her, slowly, that a steeple is a symbol that raises the church above the everyday. There is no such thing as above the everyday, Anna protested, but Braxton was thrilled about driving through downtown, counting steeples scattered like mile markers of God's progress through the city.

At that moment, one of the contractors, eavesdropping on their conversation, pointed out that a cell phone tower can be embedded inside the steeple's hollow interior – a revenue stream to offset monthly expenses.

"God is so good," said Braxton.

Damned bricklayers, thought Anna.

So she joined the church, volunteered for the building committee, and waited. One snowy March morning, she climbed up the painted ladder that was bolted to the wall, hidden behind a curtain at the front of the sanctuary.

Up on the roof, wet brush in hand, Anna pretended to paint the steeple, but was really thrusting her arm deep inside a maintenance panel, tugging at the cables, at the creeping cancer of cell phone signals spreading outward across the neighborhood. Pulling so hard that when they tore free, she lost her balance and fell, thirty feet down, bouncing off the building to the snow below.

BRAXTON STOOD on the church's front lawn, kicking at a slab of sod. Simeon stepped out of the taxi, staring up at the squat skyscrapers and parking garages surrounding the church. The last of the evening sun caught at the top corners of the tallest buildings, bright as shattering glass.

"Simeon Schaeffer?"

"Yes, sir."

"Follow me," Braxton said, leading him through the front door, down a sanctuary aisle, sitting into a pew.

"I confess, I was surprised that you accepted the internship without a visit." He spoke softly, a patient man, patient with himself, with his own voice. "Our last pastoral intern just left, and to be honest, I'm not sorry. He wasn't much for rolling up his sleeves and pitching in. But your commanding officer said you're not afraid to work."

"That's true."

"Good enough for Uncle Sam, good enough for me." He handed Simeon a key on a plastic ring. "There's a furnished bedroom in the basement, if you can call cot and shelves and hot plate furnished."

"Works for me, sir."

"Then welcome home, son."

SIMEON'S FIRST WEEK at the church was spent unpacking books into the church's library, filling shelves that smelled like new paint. One day, a man in a green jumpsuit knocked on the door.

"The preacher sent me, said you're the man to see about lawn care?" He held a folded brochure that showed a smiling employee swinging a weed eater, giving a thumbs up to the camera. "We provide superior service, without the bureaucratic bullshit of most companies." He watched Simeon's face closely, gauging how much to bid for the job based upon how much Simeon flinched at curse words.

"Do other lawn services have a lot of bureaucracy?"

"I wouldn't know," the man snapped. "I don't work for them."

Simeon held up both hands, palm forward. "You're kind to think of us," he said, "but I think we'd rather pay kids from the neighborhood. I'm sure someone in the congregation has an old push mower."

The man raised the window blinds. Three matching jumpsuits were wheeling mowers in a crisscross pattern over the grass.

"You know that's sod, right?" Simeon said, trying to speak lightly. "I don't think it has even rooted yet."

"First time is free," the man said. "Don't answer now, think on it a couple days."

As soon as he left, Simeon called the number on the brochure. He explained to the voicemail that the last thing a church needs is a service that its neighbors don't have; that a church should be like any house or laundromat or taquería on the street. The next morning, he received a letter of apology, hand-delivered by a project foreman, promising better attention to detail. In the alley behind the foreman, the jumpsuits rounded newly-planted boxwoods with roaring, gas-powered trimmers. Simeon left another voicemail and received a coupon for a 10% discount. Sent a letter, got a fruit basket. The jumpsuits had shown up every week since, to trim bushes that were already trimmed, pressure wash immaculate sidewalks.

But Simeon would never let them touch the hedge that ran alongside the alley, from the back door of the church to the street. It was an old pine hedge, thick twisted with needles and five feet tall – the only bush or tree or grass on the lot that had not been imported with the new construction. Simeon trimmed it himself, with a pair of thick kitchen scissors, sweeping the sticks into black plastic bags and carrying them, like a sweating Santa, over his shoulder to the street.

ONCE A WEEK, Simeon took three steps up to the podium, to sit behind Braxton as he preached. He watched the pews of people fighting yawns for twenty-five minutes, then took three steps back down to stand among them; to pass them on sidewalks, in schools and grocery stores, in waiting rooms and conference rooms and living rooms, anywhere they would let him in.

Some Sundays, Simeon spent the entire day in the sanctuary, in an endless round of handshakes and lunch invitations, polite questions framed as answers, answers framed as questions. The sun hit the stained glass windows, bursting the figures into reds and blues that played, slowly, across the walls as the hours passed. After the evening service and late choir practice, the sanctuary would clear and Simeon would lock the door. Then, alone at last, he would sit on the edge of the platform, praying, his hands hovering over the cloth-covered communion table. Thinking of the moment when he held the plate and cup into the air.

This was his favorite part of each service – lifting bread and wine between earth and heaven, God in the cup, his people coming forward with faces excited and unburdened and uncertain, taking something too big to hold in their hands, too big to eat in their mouths. He would pray until his head drooped; and then, instead of returning to the bare basement apartment, he would unroll a sleeping bag onto the hard pew, to sleep under the fading notes of voices that still fluttered in the rafters.

THE FIRST TIME he saw Anna, she was pushing a mop bucket through the fellowship hall, silhouetted against the French doors. One of the deacons' wives whispered for him to stop staring, telling how Anna had been an English teacher at the Christian school until a year before, until pregnancy surprised a husband who decided that he wasn't ready to be a father and vanished up I-75 toward Knoxville. How Anna offered the baby, still in her stomach, to a sterile university professor and his tragic wife, paying all of the OB and hospital costs herself, saying that the couple should save their money, invest it in a college fund. Simeon shushed the woman, saying that this should be Anna's to tell. But the woman kept talking, telling of a baby born dead, the couple left childless in the waiting room. Of Anna, spent and empty, tearing the IV out of her arm and slamming her hands in a drawer until they bled, until the nurses pushed her against the wall and filled her with Versed.

He started watching for her, greeting her in the waiting line at the church's door after every service, but she would never look up. She stood, precariously balanced, while Sunday School boys circled back for another look at the purple jelly stripes of scars on her hands. Simeon watched her walk past and out into the street, thinking: I know her doubts, her questions, her questioning of her questions.

During the service, from behind the pulpit, he could stare at her without being chided, without anyone noticing. She would sit wedged into the corner of a pew at the back of the sanctuary, her feet pulled up underneath her. She never stood with the rest of the congregation, for prayers or hymns; instead, she sat with her cheek against her arm, her mouth shaping the words utterly, ecstatically.

And then it seemed to Simeon that he saw her everywhere. Anna at every bus stop, in every street, in every store or restaurant. Maybe she had always been there, he thought, at the margins of his seeing – her long hair, her skin shades of brown on brown like a Sunday suit. Her mouth, always without makeup, the color of ripening fruit. Her hair always loose, uncombed, her clothes practical and unadorned, loose jeans and tennis shoes. As the weeks passed and the weather turned cold, wearing a knee-length coat she left unbuttoned, so it swung in arcs with each step, like heavy wings.

Even when he prayed, his eyes closed tightly, she was there; stitched into the back of his eyelids. And he couldn't help wonder if she might be the reason he had come to Chattanooga, for a girl pushing a mop bucket.

"SO, ANNA, will you listen now?" Braxton asked. "It's one thing for you to volunteer to dust and vacuum, we're very grateful. But it's quite another for you to strap on a carpenter's belt and paint the steeple. If we need that done, we've got a lawn service."

"Actually, you don't," she said, thinking of the unsigned contract she had seen on Simeon's desk, while emptying his trash cans.

"Of course we do, I've seen them. They're very professional."

"I'm sure they'd be glad to hear it."

"Don't take a tone, Anna."

Anna twisted her arm in the shoulder sling, watching him as he talked. Standing against a backdrop of flowers in the foyer, he looked like a portrait, flat and foregrounded, meticulously lined. She was aware that Simeon was in the front pew, watching them talk.

"We just don't want to see you hurt, Anna. There are so many liabilities. Although, if you would only let us pay you, put you on the payroll, then you'd be an employee. If anything happened, we could help you, better."

"I told you when I first volunteered. I can't sleep, so I might as well be useful."

"Maybe you should see a doctor. You're a young woman, you should be out having fun, not scrubbing a church."

"It's not a church, it's just a building. The people are the church."

"Yes, yes," he muttered, clipping the words. "You've said all that before. You know what I mean."

She itched; scratched at the gauze on her shoulder.

"You don't understand. Every night, after I've cleaned the whole place, I go home and sleep like an infant," she said. "Think of it like you're paying me in sleep. That's worth more, to me than a check."

"Okay, Anna. You win," he said, his mouth tight, worried for her health. "Just keep both feet on the ground."

Anna went to the maintenance closet, hanging spray bottles and rags over the rim of the wheeled trash can. Then, beginning on the top floor, she worked her way to the basement, using one hand, slower than before. Emptying bins, wiping mirrors, scratching glitter and glue from nursery tables with her fingernail. Scouring urine stains from toilet rims, bending close to dry them with a towel hanging from her waist, thinking: no servant is greater than her master.

AFTER SIX MONTHS at the church, Simeon knew all of the regulars in the congregation, so he noticed the new face right away. The boy at the back, seventeen or eighteen, with the lobe of one ear split and scabbed beneath a Band-Aid. Throughout the service, Simeon had watched him rise a half-beat after the others, fumble for a hymnal. When the congregation lined up at the communion table, he came too, waited his turn; then stepped forward with his hand outstretched, palm down. Simeon raised a soft pinch of bread to him, but the boy shook his head.

"What's the matter, Mister Reverend?" the boy asked, loudly. "Don't you want to shake my hand?"

Simeon did, and felt a folded piece of paper pushed into his palm.

"I believe in fair play," the boy said. "That makes me a better man."

Simeon watched him sidestep the table and go out the back door. He wanted to rush after, catch the boy by the shoulder and ask what he meant, but row after row of people were coming forward. Only much later, after the service, did he read the note.

Between twelve and two tonight, it said in scrawled pencil, *be ready.*

Simeon creased the paper across the middle, a new crease, as if he were folding and weakening the paper, to tear it.

AT 11:30 THAT NIGHT, Simeon closed his book and pushed it under the crinkling mattress. He pulled a sweater over his shirt and went upstairs to the small kitchen behind the fellowship hall. The automatic coffee machine chugged, filling a disposable cup so hot that the plastic shaped to his fingers.

Outside, the weather was dark, hovering between rain and snow. Simeon loved to walk the frost-slick streets at night, the wind kicking up leaves and bits of plastic, saturating his skin through the sweater. Despite warnings from Braxton that the neighborhood was not safe, he would walk through the silent downtown, exploring rocks along the river or dead parking lots sunk beside the highway, warming his hands in the trickles of heat that seeped through the windows of street-level apartments.

As he walked, he passed buildings with names chiseled into their cornerstones: entrepreneurs and philanthropists and politicians. He thought of his own name in block letters, and shuddered. Simeon liked the idea of being a nobody, of invisibility – the second superpower of every child's dreams, after flying. He had gone from seminary to the Army, becoming neither chaplain or private but something undefined, in between. Then from the Army to the pulpit, because it was a place that nobody looks, that most people ignore. And for those who do look, listen, he was duty-bound to point away from himself, past himself, to a God so enormous that he can't be seen.

A car passed, quivering the air around him. The driver's window was open an inch, the tip of a cigarette poking through, and Simeon found himself wishing that he was a smoker, too. There is something about a cigarette burning in your palm, he had once heard, that brings the world to you – as you walk down the block, someone stops you for a light or to bum one to ease their quitting cravings. When a car passes in the cold, its driver's window cracked, you know the feeling because you have done the same thing a thousand times before, and you can lift your hand to wave.

HE DOUBLED BACK up Main Street. The stores and businesses were all unlit, shuttered, except for the incandescent windows of the Mini-Mart, next door to the church. Must be up late doing inventory, Simeon thought. As he crossed the front lawn and up the steps onto the church's porch, the light from the Mart dimmed into a line of yellow, then disappeared.

The front door was unlocked; when he pulled the brass handle, Anna was there. Playing the piano, her back to him, her hair swinging side to side, marking time. He sat for a full minute, trying to block the wind coming through the open door, afraid that closing it would make too much noise. But she turned and saw him.

"Anna," he called. "I didn't know you play."

"I'm just messing around."

The sanctuary was full of the too-sweet smell of old flowers and citrus-scented cleaner.

"You should lock the door if you're here late. It's not safe."

"I never lock it."

"The nights you can't sleep?"

She laughed, a sound like a cough, like dry leaves. "I never sleep, Simeon. I clean, then I wait at the Mini-Mart until you lock up, then I let myself in. Every night, except for when you're asleep in the pews."

Simeon wondered if she had stood over him, looking down at him stretched out in the sleeping bag, his mouth gaping, snoring.

"I heard Braxton mention a doctor," he said, changing the subject.

"I went, there's nothing wrong." She brushed hair from her face with agile fingers, then tapped her forehead. "Or maybe you mean a different kind of doctor."

"No, I didn't mean that."

"I went, once," she said. "The whole time, I couldn't stop feeling bad for him. All those people sitting in the lobby, waiting to be fixed. But then I decided it's his own fault – a doctor should cut people, sew them up, do more than tell them how to feel better. Even the word sounds like a lie, a placebo: psy-chi-a-trist. All those consonants pretending to be soft, sheltering sounds."

Simeon pictured her on a leather couch, glowering.

"All he did was ask me what I feel. But I could never explain it; most of the time I don't even understand it."

"Feelings are funny like that."

"I don't think feelings are the problem," she said. "I think it's finding the words to tell them. Though words must come easily for you, being a priest."

"I'm not a priest, Anna. A priest is a holy man, set apart. I'm just a man, a pastor."

"Priest, pastor," she said. Then she hesitated, staring at the white and dark keys. "Can I ask you a question? One I've wanted to ask for a few weeks."

"Anything," he said, thinking – anything. He came around the piano, leaning on the enameled wood with his elbows.

"Why don't we have a better word for God? It's such a funny word, small as a sneeze, too manageable."

Simeon sighed. "What would you rather call him, Anna?"

"I don't know. Once upon a time, people were afraid to say his name at all."

"Maybe they weren't scared of him, but of themselves. That they would say it wrong."

"I don't think so. I've never loved anything without being afraid of it, too."

Simeon thought: so don't I, so haven't I.

"And I am afraid of him," she said. "Afraid even to talk to him – that if I do, he might take notice of me. That he might see what I think, what I want. The secret joys and shit that keep me awake all night, whispering: glory, hallelujah, but not about him." Her fingers floated above the keyboard, without pressing down. "Every morning, when I wake up, I curl under the sheets just to feel them tented over me, and I wait, and I wait. I don't even know what for."

"Sometimes we find God in small places."

She stood back from the piano. Simeon lifted her coat, holding it so she could slip her arms up the sleeves.

"Waiting is always lonely, Anna. But often, when you open your eyes, you find you aren't alone."

"And you say you're not a priest? You sure sound like one."

She half-smiled at him. The irises of her eyes, close, were brown dusted with a faint sunburst of yellow, pollen spreading on quiet water. As they walked up the aisle together, he found himself wishing, with each step, that the carpet would reach up and grab her foot, tripping her so he could catch her. When they came to the front door, she rested her hand on the handle and turned toward him.

"I want to say his name, but I can't. Will you pray for me?"

But Simeon was watching her lips. So round in thought; lightning lips, illuminating the entire sanctuary with their thundering splendor. "It's not safe for you to walk home, Anna," he said, enunciating carefully, wanting the words to be perfect. "I could walk with you."

"You know the streets are lit," she said, but Simeon, bending at the knees and angling into her, found her mouth with his. His mind raced with doing it right, thinking hard, trying to be strong and soft at the same time.

She leaned away, pushing him backward.

"You shouldn't."

The door closed between them and Simeon's forehead dropped against the cold, square window set into the wood. His breath fogged everything. He wiped it clear, watching her walk past the dim storefronts, her chin lifted, her mouth moving. Then she stumbled, sprawling to the pavement.

Simeon was halfway across the lawn when he saw Braxton hurrying out of a dark doorway across the street. By the time they reached her, Anna had pushed herself up to sitting. Braxton crouched down behind her, supporting her head with both hands.

"What have you done?" he said to Simeon, his breath short. "It's a good thing I was watching."

"Please, Braxton, help me get her up."

"Stop it, both of you," Anna said, "I'm fine."

The Mini-Mart lit the scene.

"We can take her there. Get under her arm."

But Braxton would not reach under Anna's arm to support her. He groaned, bending his hips and body away from her as he struggled to help lift her, at arm's length, slapping Simeon's hand away every time he tried to wrap her waist. Finally, she stood to her feet and they walked together to the Mini-Mart, knocked on the glass until the grocer came around the counter.

She dropped into a chair, her elbows on her knees. The front of her coat was caked with mud and slush.

"Anna," said Braxton, snapping his fingers. "When did you last eat?"

She shook her head, and the grocer reached into his display case, passing a hard-boiled egg and glass of water to her. She drank the water. Drops of sweat beaded the egg like a jewel.

Simeon nodded to the grocer. He knew the man; he had come to Sunday services for a few weeks, stopping at the front door to complain about the building, swearing that he had been in negotiations to buy the lot, to expand his store, when the old woman died. One Sunday afternoon, he stood in a congregational meeting and said that he would never come back, making a gesture of washing his hands. Simeon often ordered lunch from the Mini-Mart to support his business, but always wondered if they spat on his cold cuts when he wasn't looking.

"Anna, are you okay?" Simeon asked.

"Don't touch me."

"I won't, ever again," he said.

The colors in her eyes swirled yellow and brown, a supercell over dry and cracked landscapes.

"You don't understand, Simeon. I don't want you to, not because I don't want you to, but because I am a stain spreading from person to person, dumbly fouling everything."

"No. I am." Simeon's voice was so low that Braxton bent between them to hear it. "I thought you wanted me to, Anna. Or wouldn't mind. Or I don't know. All that talk about not being alone."

"I was talking about God. We were supposed to be talking about God."

"I was, but I was talking about me, too."

She cracked the hardboiled egg against the chair and peeled it, dropping strips of shell clicking onto the floor.

"I'm sorry, Simeon," she said. "You're not enough for me. There's no room under my sheets."

"Now hold on just a minute," Braxton said, shouldering between them. "We can't have that kind of talk."

Simeon elbowed him aside. "She doesn't mean it like that."

"But what if I do?" Anna whispered, stronger than shouting. "Did you ever think of that?"

She thought of the nights that she would sit on the floor, watching Simeon snore in a pew. With her back against the pulpit, she would arrange and rearrange the puzzle of her day, sorting through moments one by one, trying to fit them together. His snores were mumbled, gruff and yipping, but the harsh edges were smoothed in the towering ceiling of the sanctuary so that when they reached her, they were fragile, downy, with hidden melodies, almost a womanly sound. She would close her eyes into their ebb and flow, slipping into them. When they passed each other in the hallways there was always a choreography in the way he stepped past her, spoke to her, that made her want to move toward him, to let him take her in the crook of his arm, let him tuck in behind her.

"I only wanted to be close to you," he said. "I didn't want to hurt you."

"You didn't hurt me. You made my hurt disappear."

"That's a good thing," Braxton said, edging in. "So the case is closed."

"A good thing? Of course it's not," she said. "Now I'm not angry,

I'm not even scared. I'm not anything." She twisted the piece of egg in her hand. "God, I hate tripping. It's humiliating."

"Nobody likes tripping, Anna," Braxton said, nodding, trying to get both of them out the door, push them in opposite directions, each toward home.

"But maybe I should. Isn't that what saints do? A life of hurt and humiliation, waiting for God to show up."

"Who said God wants you to suffer?" Braxton asked.

"Lovers always do. And never do."

"It's not like that, Anna. He's not like that."

"How do you know, Braxton? I want to be as sure as you are. Every week, you tell us God wants us to be happy. So why am I not? Why can't your songs and prayers make me happy, why can't your beautiful building? Why can't I just say, maybe this is what love looks like?"

"I've seen you in the service," Braxton said. "You look so joyful."

"It's not joy, it's hope," she said. "The tiny hope that if your God is worth believing at all, it's only because he came into a fucked up world, to be fucked up with us, for us."

"Anna, you can't say such things," said Braxton.

"Why not? Does it scare him?"

Simeon stepped in, grasping Braxton by the shoulders and pushing him out of the way. He knelt in front Anna's chair, at her knees.

"Anna, what can I do?"

"Get up," she said, loudly, closing her fist around the egg, the white and yolk crumbling together. "A man kneels to own a woman, to taste her, to worship her. A priest should never kneel in front of a woman."

Simeon was suddenly aware that Braxton, the grocer, a boy behind the counter, were all staring at him and Anna – a tableau, a mockery of a tableau, a cartoon of desire. He glanced around at them, saying. "I'm not a priest. She shouldn't call me that."

"I'm not going to call you that, anymore, Simeon. I'm not going to call you anything."

"You tell him, sister," called the grocer.

"Anna," he whispered, "I don't know what to say."

"Good," she said, and reaching with the crumbled egg in her hand, pressed it hard against Simeon's face, smearing it across his cheek, over his mouth and chin, down the front of his sweater. A slow, bright path of color. Then she pushed out the door and was gone. As it closed behind her, a woman caught it and came into the Mini-Mart, purse in hand.

"Are you open?" she asked.

"Oh, what the hell," said the grocer. "What can I get you?"

Simeon and Braxton watched through the glass door as Anna retraced her steps up the front porch and into the church. The boy behind the counter switched on a whirling meat slicer, letting it spin to high speed with one hand on the grey. Simeon noticed, for the first time, the Band-Aid covering the split lobe of his ear.

"Hey son," the grocer called, loudly, from the register. "What do you tell a preacher with two black eyes?"

"I don't know, Dad. What?"

"Nothing. You already told him twice."

The son didn't laugh. Looking backward over his shoulder at Simeon, he heaved a ham onto the trey and pushed it toward the spinning blade.

THE WINE FILLED Simeon's mouth. He and Braxton sat in the back pew, passing an open bottle between them. At ten dollars a bottle, Simeon thought, there must be a dollar fifty left in this one.

"You stink like a fart," Braxton told him. "Go wash that egg off."

Simeon shrugged and tipped the bottle again. Anna was at the piano at the front of the sanctuary, her hands in her lap.

"Girl like that, I can't blame you for trying," Braxton whispered. "But your mistake wasn't kissing her. It was not following through." He mimed a golf swing. "Finish, man. Put a ring on it, put her in the backseat of a car and put a baby in her. If I were younger, I'd do it myself."

Simeon held up the bottle like a middle finger.

"Or don't, I don't care. Let me see that note again."

Braxton unfolded the paper on the pew beside him, smoothing it.

"You know why this is happening, Simeon? God is in the neighborhood, and people are shook up." He ran his hands through his hair, so it scattered like thoughts around his head. "We built big and we built beautiful, a place they can't disregard. And it's only going to get bigger. Anna was right – this is what love looks like." He tapped a taser, a small, square shadow in his lap. "God wants us to protect it."

"Don't say that again."

"You can't stop me, boy, any more than you can stop God. I read this note and I say, let them come. It's judgment day."

"But what if you're wrong?" Simeon asked. "What if it's something good, that's coming?"

"You pray your way, Simeon. I'll pray mine."

From her seat at the piano, Anna heard the word and thought – I can't pray, I've lost the thread. She stared at the mute keys, the tiny hammers poised to strike strings stretched to breaking, thinking about the unending rush of feeling that floods every moment, and how most of it never makes a sound. How most of it withers, without ever growing to full fruit, without being tasted.

Unlit, the sanctuary seemed enormous around her. The exposed beams of the ceiling were reversed out like gashes in the sheetrock, the only light coming from two electric candles set on each side of the pulpit – thin, twin plastic tapers topped with flame-shaped bulbs surrounding an orange filament that danced, faking fire. The candles embarrassed Anna; she thought them kitsch. She had once hidden them in the back of a maintenance closet, but Simeon found them and set them out again. He told her that they were given to the church by a family from Brazil, a husband who had made his name in Osasco as an amateur boxer, and, when he needed better medicine for his seizures, brought his wife and children northward to America. He gave the candles to the congregation on the first anniversary of their arrival in Chattanooga, telling of unwrapping them from a stained towel nightly in shadowy bus stations, to have enough light to wash their children in a water fountain. Pretending to blow them out and light them again with his finger, giggling them to sleep. Then, licking his finger by their light, carefully examining the forged passports for hints of dust and scuffs. The one thing, mile after mile, that they knew would happen for certain was the ritual search for the wall outlet, the unsteady light on the walls as they drifted to sleep.

As Anna sat at the piano, the candles suddenly, surprisingly struck her as beautiful. Their orange light dripped onto the simple tablecloth and silver cup; onto Simeon and Braxton, in the last pew. The longer she sat, staring, the more their flickering swelled and tangled in her. She thought of people lined up at the table, every Sunday, jostling as they shuffled forward together, toward bread that is bread but also flesh, wine that is not tears, but blood. And in the empty dark of the room, the faint orange light hovered over the table like a breath, and she whispered, "Oh, my God."

Simeon heard her and called out, "What's that? What'd you say?" but his voice was so jumbled that he could hardly understand himself. Braxton grabbed his arm and pulled him back to sitting.

"Easy, tiger," Braxton said.

Simeon started to call out again, but his mouth only opened and closed. If she asked me again, he thought, I could tell her different. I could tell her that if God can see through a bed sheet then we never have to be afraid, that if God can know everything then we never have to be alone, that if he can do anything but does good things instead, then maybe I can, too.

"Ask me again," he said, but it was only a slurred groan.

"Don't fall asleep, " Braxton said. "We have to stay ready."

But, I am awake, Simeon thought.

SIMEON'S FEET KICKED out in front of him, in a spasm. He wiped his chin and looked around the room. Anna was not at the piano. His head felt like it was full of wet wool. His watch said one o'clock.

The sound came again, from behind: the front door scraping the tile of the foyer. Two shapes crept into the sanctuary, wearing dark clothes and pulling ski masks down over their faces, carrying backpacks and metal canisters in their hands.

Simeon slid down to lie flat on the floor. Braxton was stretched out beside him, asleep; Simeon took the taser from the pastor's lap, hiding it behind a hymnal, then shook him softly. Braxton woke immediately, silent, aware. From the floor, Simeon could see that Anna was hiding underneath the piano; he pulled himself toward her, clutching the carpet with his fingernails, as two pairs of heavy shoes passed and stopped at the communion table.

The cup and plate clinked loudly as they dropped into a backpack, followed by the microphone.

"We'll give them to Uncle," one said, not whispering. "Think of it as back pay."

The other picked up the plastic candles, looked at them closely, then tossed them onto the floor. The electric wicks sputtered. They pulled back the tables white cloth and pulled out a case of wine, from underneath. Corks popped.

They wandered into the hallway. Simeon heard wood splintering, and dragged himself out from beneath the pews, scuttling across the open carpet to the piano. Just then the door to the hallway kicked open and they came back into the sanctuary, grunting under the weight of a television. They set it on one end of the table, picked up the metal canisters and started shaking fast, metal rattling metal. Then, a thin hiss, as they spray painted the front of the pulpit, back and forth.

"Write your name. Or better, write Uncle's. Make them pay his green jumpsuit crew to wash it clean."

Anna's mouth was inches from Simeon's hand. She started to speak, but he put his hand on her face, near her lips.

One of the men, flecked with overspatter, was swinging on a curtain, trying to tear it to the ground. The other walked, unhurried, back and forth along the wall, spraying enormous letters, pulling the ski cap off to see how high the spray could reach. It was the grocer, his chin doubled and the skin of his neck shaking.

"Hey son," he called. "What's the difference between a son of a bitch and a man of the cloth?"

The boy let go of the curtain, shrugged.

"When a son of a bitch knocks you down, he says, 'This is good for me.' When a man of the cloth does it, he says, 'This is good for you.'"

Suddenly, in the wild quiet, Simeon thought that if they showed up on the next Sunday morning, even now, he would welcome them. That if they came to the table, he would reach out, stretching his fingers past the bread and cup to touch their hands as they took it.

He stood up from underneath the piano, his fingers trailing tenderly across Anna's cheek. The boy saw him first, and stood still. The air around them was fat with wine and the synthetic mist of spray paint. His father was too busy painting on the wall to see Simeon cross and stand in front of the boy, taking his hand.

"I try to be a good person," the boy said, his lip trembling. "I try so hard."

"I do too," Simeon said. "I know exactly what you mean."

A sudden sound, a tiny chink of glass from the front of the sanctuary, and Braxton stepped out of the darkness, holding one of the electric candles. The bulb was cracked open, its filament flashing in the open air. He raised a can of spray paint from the floor and aimed for the stuttering spark. The aerosol erupted, a flame stretching three feet long, aimed toward the boy, who stood frozen to the carpet. Simeon stepped between them.

"Out of the way," Braxton shouted. Simeon didn't move, didn't speak. Braxton came closer, raising the flame between them, but the grocer and his son turned and ran up the aisle and were gone, leaving the television and the backpacks behind.

Braxton watched them go, then scanned the sanctuary's torn curtains, the spilled wine, the obscenities sketched across the walls. His face was a knot of sadness as he turned to the curtains, fanning fire until it caught and spread, quick, to the ceiling.

Simeon sprinted into the hall, remembering a fire extinguisher in the library. Tearing it from the wall, he ran back to the sanctuary, but Braxton had locked the door. He ran at it with his shoulder, then lifted the fire extinguisher over his head and brought it down on the knob, snapping it off. As he watched it roll on the floor, he remembered the master key in his pocket. He fumbled the knob back onto its stem, carefully inserting the key until it turned.

The door swung open onto pillars of fire twisting up every curtain. Braxton was standing at the communion table, his feet squared, flames pouring from each hand. The white cloth twisted in ashes.

"They're gone," Simeon yelled at Braxton, as loud as he could, batting him away and aiming the wide nozzle of the extinguisher at the table.

"I'm not finished," Braxton cried, raising both hands over his head, flames rising in twin columns. The melting plastic of the candles trailed down his fists. Simeon lowered his shoulder and, wrapping both his arms around the pastor's waist, came up under him, already running. The spray paint cans bounced away as Braxton bucked forward, kicking and slapping Simeon's back with open hands, pulling hair. He struggled up the aisle and out the front door, tumbling down the steps onto the lawn. The cold air hit them and the pastor was coughing, his face shining with sweat, the melted plastic cooling and setting around his fingers.

Simeon, lying on the grass, thought: I am not even sweating. My shirt is dry, rough as sandpaper on my chest. He felt as if his head were swelling, as if it were already twice its size. Running his hands over the parched skin of his face, he half-expected to see a camouflaged medic and thread a needle into a wriggling vein.

He stumbled up the steps, back into the burning church. The tiles of the foyer were hot under his shoes, the flowers wispy stems in their vases. Shielding his eyes against the smoke, he crawled underneath the piano with Anna just as the first piece of ceiling fell burning at the edges, trailing glowing strands of fiberglass as it spun down to the pews, where it burst in a cloud of dust.

Anna shook his arm; he opened his eyes, didn't know how long they had been there.

"Simeon, you have to get up," she said, urging him to his feet and to the back door of the sanctuary. They pushed against it, but the knob had fallen out and rolled away. She scrambled up to the pulpit, pulling him after her, backing against the wall, against the ladder that led upward to the roof.

"The roof is never locked," she shouted. She set his hands onto the rungs and pushed his thighs from beneath, hurrying him. He found himself at the top of the ladder, watching his own hands slip on the clasp, push it open.

He pulled himself onto the barren roof, inching forward. His stomach clutched under his ribs. The sky was charcoal. A circling wind pushed him over, onto his side. He could feel the heat from inside the sanctuary, through the thin black tar shingles.

"Anna?" he called. "Where are you?"

She put her hands on his neck. His pulse was shallow. "Simeon, why is your mouth blue?" She crawled over him and wrapped his arms over her own. He gripped her from behind.

"Hold onto me. Simeon, you have to keep me from slipping down the roof," she coaxed, but really she was pulling him forward, straddling the ridgepole, crawling together toward the steeple. He leaned into her, his body mirroring hers. When they reached the steeple, she pivoted underneath him, pushing his back against the painted wood.

Smoke streamed from the windows below. Houses opened onto voices, they could hear running. Anna grasped the knob of the steeple's maintenance panel and, leaning wide, looked down. She was framed by the wide span of the hedge, thirty feet below.

"Simeon, can you hear me?"

He pressed backward against the steeple, grasping blindly for her arm. Neighbors specked the street below, sirens rang from the fire hall. Anna came around him, twisting her arm to free it, but couldn't break his grip.

"We can jump, Simeon." His thumb hurt, and he saw that she was biting it. "Simeon, listen to me, I've made it before. But this time, we can aim for the hedge."

The road below was filled now with cars doubling back, groups of people bunched on the lawn. Someone screamed, pointing at them. Simeon held on to her neck as hard he could.

"Stop it, Simeon," she shouted. "You're hurting me."

"I'm not hurting you, Anna," he said, "I'm saving you."

She stopped twisting against him and, suddenly slow, pulled in close. She arched her face upward to his.

"No, Simeon, you aren't."

Her lips touched his forehead, lightly. Then she coiled her hands and around his wrists and, putting one foot on each side of his body, flat against the steeple, leaned backward. He leaned forward to catch her, and she pulled him over. Her hair ballooned around them both. His hands shook loose, flapping featherless at the air. Shouts from below cut off in a surge of wind. The hedge expanded beneath them, growing in detail until it opened, fringed in soft green, to take her. Then it took him, too, the tender needles cushioning before the branches beneath knocked the wind out of his chest.

Anna was surrounded by hands. She watched them reach into the hedge toward her, lift and shift her, sliding her out between the branches. They carried her across the lawn, away from the building, past where Simeon lay. Her tongue fumbled the edge of a broken tooth; she spat red. Sleepy flakes of ash dropped like warm snow in the cold, soundless, slight. People in winter coats and pajamas surrounded them, hurrying from all sides to bring blankets and bottled water.

She watched an old woman from the neighborhood, whom she recognized from Sunday services but whose name she didn't know, cross the road as fast as she could. The woman wrapped Anna in a tattered quilt.

"You okay, honey?" she asked, helping Anna to her feet, folding a corner of the quilt to wipe her face. Taking her hand, she led Anna past the edge of the crowd, stopping by reflex at the street's edge to look both ways.

An ambulance spun to a stop and Anna turned back to look for Simeon. As she watched, someone pushed a bottle of water into his limp hand. Others pulled off his sweater and unbuttoned his shirt, tugged at his pants, even the white briefs. They folded the clothes and bunched them under his head. A man removed his coat to cover Simeon's nakedness as they knelt, in close, hands full of dirty snow, cooling his forehead, his heaving chest.

At the far side of the lawn, flaming drops of tar fell from the roof, splashing the grass. A window split and a heavy wooden beam burst through the glass and bricks, folding the wall around it, bringing it down. But as it fell, to Anna it seemed that the wood and glass and bricks stopped short, before they hit the ground, shifting to form new and beautiful configurations in the air.

THE REASON THAT JOHANNA, at 23, was still a virgin was because of her grandmother. On her twelfth Christmas, the old lady had pulled her aside, brushing the hair back from her ear to whisper that the first time a woman takes off her clothes in front of a man, she always breaks wind. Loud and clear as a foghorn at dawn – the Big Bang, she called it. Of course, in Johanna's case it might not happen, her grandmother said, as she disappeared into the crowded family room. But all through school and university, every time poor Johanna held a boy close in a dark corner, she clenched her backside tight.

On her wedding night she told Thomas, asked him. Said she'd spent her teenage years watching scenes of young love in movies, the television volume turned as high as it would go, waiting for the telltale rumble. But she could never be sure. Was that noise a bedspring? A bass note in the sound track? She would focus on the boy's face on screen, waiting for his nose to crinkle.

Thomas told her that he wouldn't care, that he didn't care. But she only wanted him to say it wouldn't happen.

"So let's find out," he said, laughing, already naked and fumbling at her clasps. Her face flushed upward from the neck and she pushed him sprawling out of the bed, backward onto the floor. She laughed, too, as if a string linked her laugh to his, pulling it out of her. But she also reached, wildly, and finding the alarm clock, threw it hard. The plug jerked out of the outlet as it flew, the undulating cord trailing. He watched it come, still laughing, rolling out of the way as it smashed against the wall in a scatter of plastic and metal coils.

That was one week ago, in a hotel room a block from the church, one hour after the cake and best wishes and rice floated in the air around them.

IT IS THREE O'CLOCK in the morning, and Thomas is standing at the open window of a Guangzhou hotel room, in his underwear. He is watching through the trees of the garden for glimpses of crowds. Over the city's chatter of two-stroke motors and all-hours construction and the animal screeches of buses, the chanting from the street below rises and falls like a vinyl record spun fast, slow, fast against the needle.

Johanna is on the bed, awake, wearing only Thomas' tee shirt. She keeps saying that the night could be more alive, faster, bolder, brighter if they were out in the streets, too, among the crowds. The more people, the more possible; but here in the hotel room, there are only two of them. Thomas' face grows hot, despite the breeze coming off the high garden waterfall.

"Isn't that the point of a honeymoon?"

"One of many, I suppose. But would it kill us to go out?"

"It might, Johanna. For God's sake, they put guards with guns at the door. They're trying to protect us."

"They just don't want the hotel's name in the papers," she says. "You could protect me. I could ride on your back."

"Like a mule."

"That's right. Like a big, handsome mule."

The air conditioning unit gasps, useless, from the window. Johanna sits up, her legs crossed off the bed, like she is fishing in the carpet with her toes. As they talk, she hardly looks up from her mobile phone, where her fingers sketch words and doodles on the flat illuminated screen. Her eyes follow the motion of her fingertips, and Thomas wonders if she is trying to lure him back into bed. But she is thinking about airline timetables and lost days.

"Our flight leaves tomorrow, eleven hours to Los Angeles. We should go to the Consulate, get them to help us."

"Help us with what? Sightseeing?" he says. "Anyway, none of the taxis would take us."

"Why not? The news said only police cars and fire engines are being attacked."

"You don't know that's true."

"You don't know it's not."

She lies back on the bed, spread out like a treasure map. Her face is covered in tiny freckles, chocolate pinpricks on her skin that look, at a glance, like acne or hives. Thomas loves to lie close to her, trying to decipher patterns and hidden meanings. She looks up at him.

"You got lucky," she says, watching him watch her. "Stuck in a honeymoon suite while the world riots outside. Can't see the sights, can't go shopping. What to do? Okay, we did that. What to do, next? We did that, too."

For a moment he thinks she is blushing, but then he remembers the sunburn, that his face is as red as hers. The night they arrived in China, nearly a week ago, the first attacks on the police happened a few blocks over from their hotel and the doors had been locked ever since.

Five days of the hotel's room service, of wandering the gift shop, reception halls, dusty service corridors behind the kitchens where young men cut fish and vegetables for the buffet. Every afternoon on the pool deck, their skin going red, then tan, then red again.

"But now you're stuck with a bored bride, and every day the room feels smaller than it did the day before, and it's egg frittata for breakfast, again, and just because they call it a honeymoon, honey, that doesn't mean it's always sweet."

She smiles at him, knowing that the ruddy tan looks good on her. Knowing that the morning sweat and unwashed hair only highlight her lovely face, the power of the quick tips of her fingers tracing across the surface of his eyes.

"I'm ruining everything," she teases, tests. "We should just turn on the TV and become an old married couple, right now."

"It doesn't matter," Thomas says, "it's nothing." Thinking how when the Chinese say, It's nothing, they sound like they mean it. All the stewardesses and salespeople and doormen chiming the words, dismissing gratitude. This is what I do, who I am. No need for thanks.

She stands and crosses to him, the cotton tee shirt draping and peaking on her. She buries her face in his shoulder and bites, too hard, her teeth bunching his skin. Steps back to look where she bit, the wet hoop mark from her teeth. She grins up at him, then suddenly looks through the open window.

"What's that noise?" she says, as though until that moment she heard only her own voice talking. Through the window, past the trees and flowers and koi pond below, come little bursts like distant gunfire.

"It's tree frogs, remember?"

When the airport shuttle had rolled into to the hotel's circle drive, the pavement had been covered in frogs – brown, bouncing dots, their throaty rattling calls punctuated by the sound, every few seconds, of one of them popping under the tires. The doorman had apologized in English, explaining that a long-time guest of the hotel had bought a dozen of the frogs in Hong Kong as a present for a local mistress; but she, saying that she wanted a child instead of childish gifts, had tossed them out of the window. Within weeks, the frogs filled the trees. Every so often, he said, the hotel brings in chemical exterminators, but the problem has become so bad that management fears they will have to close the garden, raze and rebuild it.

"It can't be frogs," Johanna says, listening to the harsh, reedy calls. "It doesn't sound like anything alive. It sounds like kids sword fighting with sticks, like a mob bashing police cars with rakes and brooms. Or guns, out beyond the garden wall."

She peers through the open window, searching for a one-to-one ratio between what she believes and what she knows. The softness of the lamp hangs on her skin. The collar of Thomas' tee shirt drapes wide at her neck, showing the sweet sweep down to her shoulders, the collarbones pooling shadow. Her summer tan in the night room, winter-white strap lines peeking out. She sees him looking at her and pulls the curtain closed, stepping into him again. He places his hands on either side of her face, but she reaches upward, guiding them over her ears to the top of her head. Resting his hands there, under her own, like a blessing, like an offering, like a claim.

HE WEARS JOHANNA on his back, down the escalator and into the lobby. She is wearing sweatpants and a cardigan over the tee shirt. Her legs wrap him, relaxed, trusting his grip, and Thomas thinks how she is smaller than she looks, easier to carry than he had imagined.

He walks down the escalator, ignoring the black and yellow signs that tell him, in English, to hold the handrail. The bright lobby lights come up slowly to meet them, reflected from the polished floor and the reception desk and the ten-foot sprays of plastic flowers and gold leaf of the ceiling. Hostesses in white collared shirts and black flats nod politely, the arches of their feet turned flat from standing all day.

Even before they step off of the elevator, Thomas can hear the huddled group crying softly from the long benches in the tea lounge. Five or six couples, obviously American in their khaki shorts and print skirts, holding screaming Chinese toddlers perched on hips or bouncing on knees.

They were there, in the same corner, when Thomas and Johanna checked in; the concierge explained that the hotel offers special rates to Americans because hundreds pass through each year, staying at the hotel for a week while waiting their turn at the Consulate, for a visa for their newly adopted son or daughter. The hotel is surrounded with branches of U.S. banks, with shops selling disposable diapers and Cheerios; the staff are trained in American lullabies and infant CPR. Every time Thomas and Johanna had come downstairs, the group had been sitting close to the doors, as if waiting for the Army to show up.

Thomas walks the gilt lobby, Johanna still on his back. The entrance doors are shuttered and hung with paper signs warning about the armed guards and 24-hour curfew. The other hotel guests, in town from Frankfurt or Dubai or Chicago for trade fairs, are spread throughout the tea lounge in champagne clusters of two and three, chatting up lobby prostitutes who hope for one more trick before daybreak. The Cantonese executives with them talk in loud, tonal, dogmatic voices, making the huddled Americans even more nervous.

Outside, the dark night is warm, as it has been all week. Music is playing in the brightly lit garden, the volume turned up louder than the clacking noise of the frogs and the yellow tock of tennis balls on clay courts.

Thomas sets Johanna down at a table. Behind her is a long buffet counter of glistening croissants and frittatas, bright fruit and sweating bamboo dumpling steamers. Painted on the wall behind the buffet is a fresco of women sketched in simple strokes – dancing in a row, lifting their heels out of slippers, the black dashes of their eyes cut low, one hand stretching toward the next, never touching.

A bartender appears out of nowhere and hovers until they order drinks. While they wait, Thomas runs his hand over the tabletop. It is polished concrete, a dusty tint just missing white, smooth but dry under his palm, and he thinks that, in spite of the high waterfall just outside the open French doors, and the hundred fountains in front of branded stores, and the wide proud Pearl River, the whole city feels dry, indescribably dry. As if, as a service to tourists, giant unseen machines sucked it clear of all moisture. When the bartender brings his drink, Thomas thinks that if he were to raise it over his head and smash it down on the tabletop, he could watch the concrete suck up the liquid – suck even the shards of glass like tiny, pointed drops of water immediately away, leaving no stain.

Johanna elbows him softly, pointing. In the corner, one of the couples is bent over a tangle of blankets. All of the color fades out of a crease in the woman's forehead as fold of blanket slips and Thomas sees a baby's head arch backward at the neck, stiff as stone. The father sits, cross-legged, on the floor in front of them, clapping his hands uselessly, trying to make the baby stop crying.

"You don't understand, Andy," the wife says loudly. "How could you possibly understand?"

As Andy takes the bundle into his lap, the blanket drops again, falling away from the child's face. A half-inch gap is missing out of its upper lip, with no gum behind, only the red-black, empty mouth. The flaring upper lip folds, on one side, neatly up into a nostril, and twisted teeth jut into sight, into the fluttering sound of its crying.

"That poor boy, his poor parents," Johanna whispers.

"I wish I could explain it, Andy. It's like my own body is against me. You'd think after fifteen years, I'd be used to it."

"Maybe I could get you something."

"What would you get me? There's nothing for it."

"I don't know." The baby twists in his arms. "Maybe some Advil."

He leans toward her but she is beyond him, holding onto her wordless ache. She stands up and walks to the escalator.

"Wait, I'll come with you," Andy says, scrambling for the stroller and toys. The baby screams louder, tears and mucus smearing across its cheeks and into the open mouth.

"No, you stay here." Her hand grips white around the handrail as she ascends backward, facing into the lobby. The escalator takes her past an open window and she points outside. "And another thing," she says loudly. "Don't tell me that isn't gunfire."

"They told us already, it's frogs. In the garden," Andy says back, embarrassed.

"I don't believe you," she shouts. Heads turn, watching her rise slowly backward. "Five days of riots, and now they've got machine guns."

"Not guns. Tree frogs, from Hong Kong," says the concierge from the desk, speaking into a hidden microphone. "Very popular, very strange, very cute. Only they reproduce so fast. If they bother you, may I close the window?"

Thomas watches as the woman disappears upward, but Johanna is watching the baby's crying face, arched against Andy's stomach. Andy sees her staring and frowns.

"Johanna, don't," Thomas whispers but she is already on her feet, walking toward the man and baby. Thomas follows. Closer, Andy's face is as tired and blotched as the baby's.

"You two married?" Andy asks.

"For one week," Johanna answers, sitting on the floor beside him.

"I've been married ten years. But I think it might be over." The baby is still crying loudly from his lap; he strings words together, talking loud and fast despite a Southern drawl. "She wants a baby but she can't." He points at the child. "So we did this. But I don't think she's happy with how it's turning out."

"Give it some time."

"That's what I've been saying. For years. The problem is, she thinks she can have her own, because she still cramps every month, and why would God do that to her, she says, if not for a reason. But I got tested. It's not my fault. Only, I don't have the heart to tell her." He sighs, looking at the child. "My guess is she'll try with someone else."

Johanna smiles at him, but he looks away from her, not wanting to receive it.

"You want to hear a joke?" he asks. "You know why we had to adopt a Chinese kid?"

"I'm sure I don't," Johanna says, playing along.

"Because two whites can't make a wong."

Johanna makes a face.

"It's not funny, I know," Andy says. "I thought of it last night, when he wouldn't stop crying, hour after hour. I had to tell someone. I've always been like that, I can't sit on a joke, even a bad one." He folds the blanket over the child's wailing, tremulous, twittering mouth. "It's who I am. If people don't like me for me, I'm sorry. I have good days, too."

Thomas wants to tug her sleeve, to pull her away, to say you don't know these people. But Johanna asks, "Where are you from?"

The man's expression wrinkles, closes. "Why would you ask me that? You think I'm a racist," he says. "How could I be? I just flew halfway around the world for a baby."

"I never said that. I just want to know."

He shifts against the carpet. "Tennessee."

"I've never been to Tennessee. Do you miss it?" Johanna asks. She leans back against a wall, folding one leg over the other. Thomas walks to the French doors, wishing his wife would follow him away from this man, from this child with its gaping, alien, aberrant mouth.

"Chattanooga is a little downtown, nestled between the mountains and the river. The river splits the city, with shops on one side and high-rise offices on the other. And right in the middle of the river is an island. Sprawling and green."

"People live on it?"

"There's nothing on it. Just trees and muddy beaches, an old Scout lodge. It was owned by a rich family until they gave it to a mayor and he put their name on it, on the map. As kids, we used to steal out there to throw rocks at tourists boats. And skinny dip."

Johanna laughs, as if on cue. "I bet loads of people saw."

"Nobody saw us, nobody was watching. We would hide in the bushes at the waterline and watch life hurry by on shore." He glances at the shining lobby clock. "It's nearly four in the afternoon there."

"Other side of the world," Johanna says, "other side of the clock."

"Right now, men are dropping ice cubes into highballs, for women on restaurant patios. Moms with strollers are crossing the walking bridge. Paddles knock against canoes, wood on wood, as barges pass in the channel. Fog is rolling down from the mountains and up the river. People sit in coffee shops, reading the Bible and Neil Gaiman. The air is wet and heavy. Raindrops. A bird."

China has raindrops, Thomas thinks, China has birds. But Johanna says, "Your son will love it."

"Before I was born, the foundries and railroads were booming. We had the dirtiest air in America, from all that coal. They say it never snowed, not even in the mountains. There was too much pollution, too much crap in the air for flakes to form."

Johanna pantomimes disbelief, vaudevillian. "Maybe it's not the air that's full of crap."

He laughs broadly, patting the baby's back. "It snows now. The foundries dried up and moved away, leaving downtown rusting and vacant. But the air was cleaner. We could start building back better. And today, you can eat the snow."

Standing at the open doors, Thomas watches through the glass as the waterfall, tumbling white from fifty feet overhead, trails away into a trickle. Without the sound of its hidden pumps and gears, of water bouncing down the steep false rock face into the pond below, the music seems louder. The pond drains in seconds, leaving orange and yellow koi flopping against a blue plastic liner. A man in overall waders, a long-handled net in his hand, appears and walks among the fish, scooping and flipping them into a wheeled tank. Another follows with a push broom and a spray bottle of bleach, scrubbing away algae.

Thomas walks through the French doors, staring up at the turned-off waterfall, stepping out onto the pond liner. The man with the fish net waves him back but Thomas replies, "It's okay, I'm okay," and the man returns to the fish. Beyond him, no longer hidden by the falling water, a path is cut into the flowering bushes, leading down to the outer wall of the garden. Even from the pond, Thomas can see an iron service gate, open to the street.

Thomas hurries back into the hotel lobby, taking Johanna's hand and pulling her away from Andy, from the child's split and wailing mouth, through the doors.

THE UPTURNED LEAVES of plants are still misty from the falls. At first, the path looks empty except for surprising shapes cast by the hotel lights, but as they move deeper along the path, they step over broken pots and statuary, dropped garden tools, bloated plastic bags filled with the shadows of rotting fish. White PVC pipes and hoses jut out of the ground. Fruiting trees hang low; Johanna reaches up to touch lychee and wampee as they pass. Everywhere on the ground, fruit lies split and flattened, its juice running, drying sticky.

They come through the iron gate and find themselves on a pedestrian overpass, surrounded by people. Below them is a six-lane highway, with row upon row of more people, standing, waiting under ghostly faces that watch through twenty floors of smudged windows. A light post has been torn down, its wires splayed against the sidewalk, and groups of people shift in patches, flashlights bobbing.

Johanna holds tightly to Thomas' arm as they edge along the wall and climb onto a stack of crates. People are everywhere on the highway below, standing on the concrete median, sitting on the white dashed lines, holding a hemp rope across all six lanes.

Suddenly, fifty yards ahead, the crowd unzips around a man running with a rock in his hand, his arm cocked back, a rusty motor scooter thumping alongside him; he lobs the rock out of sight over the crowd, then jumps onto the back of the scooter and disappears. A wave of whistles and shouts goes up with a scurry of clapping, then dies again into watching, waiting.

"Why are they so angry?" Thomas says, half to himself.

"I heard that a policeman shoved a pregnant street vendor."

"What happened?"

"Her husband fought back. All of these people are migrant workers from his province, come out to protest."

"I mean, what happened to the woman, to her baby?"

"Oh," Johanna says. "I don't know."

A man standing on the median holds up a penlight, a signal or symbol that Thomas doesn't know. Ahead, a semi trailer truck creeps forward, flashing its headlights. The crowd backs away in front of it, bodies folding upon bodies until the truck rolls to a stop, gunning its engines.

A man jumps onto the hood and smacks the windshield with the flat of his hand. Another follows. The truck's horn blasts and the crowd closes around it like a fist, pushing against the cab, rocking it side to side, the headlights swaying, until its gears grind and it reverses slowly back to the far side of the bridge. The crowd shouts and cheers, louder and longer than before.

"Hell yeah!" Thomas shouts, clapping along. "It didn't have a chance, not with so many of them." Around them, people are stamping and cheering, the noise ricocheting off the walls, the street, the sky. He yells to Johanna, inches from his face: "Have you ever seen anything like that?" He stamps the crate with his foot, rocking it, and shouts again.

The air is thick with sharp smells from the shops and alleys, with people breathing, yelling together, words he doesn't understand. A few of the people close by are nodding and touching him on the chest, touching Johanna on the shoulders and back as she clings to his arm. The truck backs out of sight. The crowd lets it go.

"I would have done the same thing," Thomas shouts to Johanna. "If someone pushed you down with a baby inside you, I would hit back. I would call everyone I know, to come with me, to strike down the hand that touched you."

Johanna is pulling at him, yelling into his ear but he can't hear her, can't make out the words, until her nails bite through his sleeve. He turns to face her. She is sobbing.

"Please, please stop," she says, over and over. Her face is dim and faded in the dark, tears striping the light from the shops and buildings around. "Please take me back."

"But you were right, Johanna," he shouts. "We're fine, we'll be fine. We can slip into the crowd, come back later tonight, or even tomorrow. Nobody will know."

"What if I can't hold onto you?"

"You can. I can."

"What if you can't?"

"But this is what you wanted."

"I don't want it anymore." She says it as if she didn't have a choice. "I hate it, and I'll hate you if you make me go."

She pulls him down off the crates and in through the gate, closing it behind them. He lets her lead him up the path. Overhead, the waterfall comes on with a whistle of air in the pipes, the first drops soaring through the air toward the shallow pond, so they have to hurry, the water filling around their shoes. As they cross, a web of reflected light flickers over their faces, and the hollow sound of the frogs springs up on every side.

Inside, the lobby is quiet. The clock shows almost five in the morning. Stooped women are mopping the floors with hand rags. The American parents have gone upstairs to order room service for dinner, pizza or hamburgers, trying to keep their internal clocks set to U.S. time. But with nobody to wake him, Andy is sleeping in the corner, tipped over on the couch. The child is crawling at his feet, trailing the blanket.

Johanna sits at a table, without a word. Thomas goes to the buffet and walks its length with a paper napkin in his hand, opening chafing dishes to peek inside. He chooses a slice of frittata and sits across from Johanna. Cups the napkin under his chin, takes a bite, chews slowly, then takes another. When he finishes, he crosses to the buffet again before seeing that the baby is watching him from the floor. The slitted eyelids, black pools of pupils, and the mouth all swivel, following Thomas' hand.

Thomas folds another piece of frittata in the napkin and comes close; the child watches warily, out of the side of his eyes, not moving, as if he had learned to sit still and unnoticed, seeing the world from below, waiting in a bubble of quiet. But as Thomas comes within arm's reach, he lifts his chin.

The mouth opens, the lips spreading too wide. Thomas hesitates, looking at the loose flaps of skin, the crooked teeth, then sits on the floor and pulls off a piece of the frittata with his fingers. The baby takes it in his hand and pushes it into his mouth, his whole hand following after, trying to push the food back to swallow it, but missing. Thomas bends forward, his forehead almost touching the carpet; sees the food drift upward, through the gaped palate, until the tongue works bits of egg out through both nostrils.

Thomas wipes it away, flinging it yellow across the floor. He lays one hand on the baby's head and takes another bite, chews it and spits it into his own hand, rolling it tenderly between his fingers, then pushes it into the child's mouth. Working by feel, his fingers slip up into the gap in the child's lip, the skin closing around it like a wound. The baby swallows the frittata and suckles at Thomas' finger, trying to draw milk from it.

"Hold on, fella. I'm not your mother," Thomas says and takes another bite, chews it.

Andy stirs above him and sees Thomas crouching on the floor. "What the hell?" he starts, angry, shrill. "What are you doing to my son?"

"Quiet," says a voice at Thomas' shoulder. He didn't know she was watching. "Don't say a word, Andy," she says. "Just watch."

Thomas bites, then chews, then shows the small ball of mash in his palm. "Like this," he says and gently sets it at the back of the child's teeth, plugging the gap in the palate until the boy swallows.

He hands the napkin to Andy, who kneels on the floor. They watch as Andy takes a bite and chews, stroking his son's face and spitting into his hand. He does not turn to thank Thomas and Johanna as they back away, breaking into a run halfway up the escalator.

At the landing, they nearly collide with a group of men in suits, who step aside to avoid them. They come around the landing and onto the next escalator, slowing now, each reaching for the other's hand as they run.

MARTIN GEYER, sixty-five, from Cambridge, Mass., only just retired from years of traveling to trade shows, stirs against the sheets. He wonders if he should sit up, should look see what waked him, but sleep still creeps the room around him, saturating the unmoving air. He forces his eyes open, feeling that he's missed something.

"Did you say something?" he whispers, reaching to touch his wife. After twenty-seven years of flying to expos in Guangzhou, in the first month of his retirement he has brought Beatrice to see the city he knows so well.

She rearranges her body into a warm spot in the blankets.

"It was that young couple," she says. "The ones who are always in the lobby in their pajamas."

"And I was hoping to sleep in. Did they wake you, too?"

"I wasn't asleep."

Martin shifts his leg so it touches her thigh; the soft skin wrapped in a loose nightgown that warms quickly against him.

"The light on the landing is out," she says.

"We should tell the staff," he mumbles. "These damned escalators are dangerous enough as it is."

"Yes. We'll mention it to the front desk."

He stirs again. "I know the ones you mean. They're young. Are they married?"

"Who knows, these days."

"But they're so young."

"They wouldn't be the first."

She presses the soft underside of her foot against his, and they both lay silent for a long time.

"But is everyone all right?" he says, suddenly. "I heard a noise. Did somebody fall?"

"No, nobody's hurt. Go back to sleep, you kind, old man."

Once he is snoring, Beatrice speaks, slowing her voice in tempo with his breathing, talking herself to sleep, as she does every night.

"I was up for a glass of water. I heard voices from the hallway and went to the peephole. They were standing in the dark, breathing fast, breathing hard, like they had been running. Resting, each with one hand on the wall beside our door. I could see their shapes so clearly. He pushed against her, not hard, but like he was covering her, and she slipped her hand into his waistband. I looked away, afraid they might hear me, but after a minute I looked again. They hadn't moved. I could see the shape of them against the light, but couldn't see their faces. Then he bent, picked her up onto his back, and began walking up the dark escalator, her legs swinging in the air as they went."

acknowledgements

The Empress of the Blues, Bessie Smith, wrote "Thinking Blues," the song that opened my eyes to home. "Cantata 82" is named for Bach's "Ich Habe Genug," BWV 82 in the Schmieder catalogue. In "East Coker," T.S. Eliot wrote lines that shifted into "The Houses Under the Sea, the Dancers Under the Hill." The Georges Simenon books referenced are *Maigrets*; Neil Gaiman's is *American Gods*; the basketball scene in "Patete" samples James Baldwin's timeless description of Sonny on stage.

With thanks to Dr. Mary McCampbell, Sybil Baker, Phillip Johnston, Ali DuPey, Lacie Stone, Eliza Hill, Madison Cumbee, Robb Ludwick, Jotham Burrello and the Yale Writers' Conference. To Antqunisha, Areon, Cynthia, Erianna, Eric, Ivan, Jakiryeon, LeBrisha, Lexi, Monica, Prianna, Scyhuler, and Teryan, for working so hard at the lit mag. To Michael Hendrix, Ben Horner, Mandy Lamb Meredith, Nick DuPey, Liz Tapp, Roby Isaac, Joseph Shipp, and Beth Joseph, for collaborating on the print version; to Paul Rustand for designing the cover.

Thanks also to the Lyndhurst Foundation, who supported the writing of these stories with a MakeWork grant. To Chad at C&R Press, for introducing himself after a reading, for his relentless love of words, and for making these stories a small part of his great work. Most of all, to Krista Gerow Ludwick, Ada Matthews, Evelyn Jane and Mathilda Pinyi, for everything.

www.ingramcontent.com/pod-product-compliance
Lightning Source LLC
Chambersburg PA
CBHW051303250626
47155CB00009B/3415